If I Should Die

Crime After Crime, Volume 3

M K Farrar and M A Comley

Published by Warwick House Press, 2020.

This is a work of fiction. Similarities to real people, places, or events are entirely coincidental.

IF I SHOULD DIE

First edition. January 28, 2020.

Copyright © 2020 M K Farrar and M A Comley.

ISBN: 979-8607768126

Written by M K Farrar and M A Comley.

Prologue

The figure was a mere spot in the distance.

Bent against the sloping hillside, the weight of their pack increasing their stoop, they plodded on, unaware they were being followed.

I paused long enough to catch my breath and admire the view. It was truly beautiful out here. Heavy white clouds gathered around the mountain peak, thick and lustrous in the blue of the sky. High overhead, a couple of buzzards used the thermals to soar.

The isolation was what these people loved, which worked perfectly for me.

The stark landscape of the Scottish Highlands was as capable of killing as I was. When the sun shone, the rolling hills and glasslike water of the lochs was enough to make you catch your breath, but in the distance were the jagged mountains that would be topped with snow in the winter months. Ten people had died during the previous winter season, and now, though it was almost summer, I intended to add some more to the body count.

I wasn't a young man any longer.

I'd felt the passing of time more acutely these past couple of years. My own mortality wasn't something I'd ever given much thought to. I was someone who took life, not someone who had it taken. But lately, I couldn't deny that I was getting older. My body ached in a way it never had. My teeth had grown weaker. My hair appeared thinner in certain lights.

Time was running out.

And with that acknowledgement came panic. I still hadn't fulfilled my full potential. The drive within me was like a wave, peaks of intense highs and desires and needs I couldn't control, followed by troughs where I felt like I was in a time of hibernation, resting and growing stronger. My most recent period of inactivity had been longer than any previously, and before I'd realised it, years had passed. What was becoming of me? Had I lost my touch? I'd thought perhaps I had, and maybe something had changed within me. It was only normal for drives to adjust within a man once he'd grown older. Hormones affected virility and muscle strength in the same way it had my teeth and hair, and I wondered if the passion had simply gone.

But then I woke one morning, and something had shifted. A new fire had ignited within me, a switch flicked on, waking me from my slumber. And at that moment I realised nothing had changed. I'd needed the extended rest because this would be bigger than anything else. The challenge and risks far greater.

I was a patient man. I'd proven that to myself over the years. In fact, I enjoyed the wait. Making things last longer allowed me to savour them fully, but it did also mean that when they were over, the trough hit me even harder. It was a kind of mourning, I believed. Something—someone—who had taken up such a huge part of my life, someone I'd devoted all my attention and focus towards, was no longer there, and I was grieving that loss. Ha! How they would react if I tried to imply that they should be grateful for the attention I'd given them. How many other men did that? But did I ever get a word of thanks? Of course not.

I wondered if they ever missed me, too?

I'd been tempted to go back, but it was never worth the risk. One thing I had that was stronger than my desire to cause pain was my own sense of self-preservation. I had no intention of languishing away in prison for years. I'd already had a taster of what that was like, and I'd rather die than repeat it.

Out here, the space helped me think. I could literally be anyone I wanted to be. People recognised me as one of their own, and drew me into their small gatherings, cosying up in the remote pubs they came across, or camping when the weather was good. There was none of the suspicion of the cities, where everyone automatically closed up if a stranger spoke to them. Things had grown even worse in recent years. Social media hadn't helped with that. Crime was no more prevalent than it had been thirty years ago, but everyone knew about it now. The world felt like a more dangerous place, and the population reacted as such.

Of course, they had every right to be mistrustful of me, and they were right to be wary, but out here, people didn't act that way. The walking boots, the poles, the backpack all signalled we were the same sort of ilk. Part of a club.

Then they let down their guard.

I was always amazed at the amount some individuals told strangers about their lives. Those with a family, or work they needed to get back to, or friends they were meeting along the route would be an instant no for me. I had to be sure whoever I chose wouldn't be missed.

These were the only times I ever really felt anything. The rest of the time I was like a ghost inside a human suit, reacting to things around me in a way I felt someone would if they were alive. Human. Real. I wore a mask, and I was good at it. I knew how to laugh and smile in all the right places, had learned how to mirror their body language to make them feel more comfortable. This wasn't something I'd studied; I'd fallen into it naturally. It was ironic that the thing I found most natural to do—act like a normal human being—wasn't natural to me at all.

I continued to track my target, my feet taking the same steps his had only minutes earlier. It was rough terrain, but these past few weeks had increased my fitness, allowing me to traipse up the incline without getting too puffed out.

If the person turned, perhaps taking in the view of the rolling mountains, then I would be spotted. Not that it mattered too much. Even though we were a day or two from civilisation, people often took similar routes. Perhaps he would find it strange that I hadn't mentioned following the same path a couple of evenings ago, when we'd discussed our hikes while nursing a pint of ale in one of the remote pubs, but I could easily have had a change of heart. Being seen wouldn't stop me doing what I had planned.

The figure vanished over the top of the hill, disappearing into the valley beyond. I relaxed a fraction, my shoulders dropping, breath huffing from my lungs. The valley would be better, I decided. Less exposed.

I continued my climb to the top until I reached the peak. From this vantage point, I was able to see over the other side. Excitement grew inside me. The anticipation was the only time my heart ever raced. Even during the killing, I was calm, and afterwards, too.

I paused.

He was closer than I'd expected. He must have rested on the other side of the ridge, when he'd been just out of view, catching his breath after the steep climb or simply taking in the vista. Only now he was heading downhill, and his momentum had increased. I wanted to catch up before he reached the bottom.

Staying as light on my feet as it was possible for a full-grown man to manage, I followed him down.

I was a mere couple of feet away when he either heard or sensed my presence. His pace slowed, and he glanced over his shoulder.

A flash of recognition lit the man's eyes, but the light was quickly dulled by confusion. He was fighting that instinct to be polite, despite deep down knowing something wasn't quite right. He didn't stop fully, but he turned in my direction and slowed enough to let me catch up, so he was now almost walking backwards.

"Oh, hello again!" he said, his tone jovial. "I almost didn't hear you there. I thought you weren't—"

I moved quickly, pulling the knife from my pocket and opening it with a flick of my wrist. I took another couple of steps, closing the gap between us.

My soon-to-be victim reared back, but not quickly enough. I swung my arm, bringing the blade around in an arc. Sharp metal met with firm flesh, and the flesh lost. The knife sank in deep, and the surprise and confusion in the man's eyes flashed to fear and pain.

It wouldn't have mattered if he'd screamed. There was no one around to hear him.

I stepped back, and my victim dropped to his knees.

Despite the blade sticking out of his neck, the man crawled away, somehow knowing that putting distance between himself and the person who'd stabbed him was more important than yanking the knife from his body.

I watched with wry amusement. Where did he even think he was going? There was nothing and nobody out here—no one for him to crawl to for help. Did he realise how slowly he was moving? Each lift and bend of a knee or reach of a hand was in slow motion, as though he was struggling through water. The valley we were in now meant the only way out was if he climbed one of the steep hillsides to the top, and it was hard work even when you didn't have a knife protruding from your throat. He didn't stand a chance.

Two paces brought me back in line with him.

"It's okay." I kept my voice calm, soothing. "You don't have to keep fighting now. You can rest."

A gurgling whine of fear escaped him, but, for some reason, my words didn't have the desired effect, and he increased his efforts to get away.

His arm buckled under his body, and he slumped forwards, his face planting in the gorse and mud, his backside still in the air. It wasn't a dignified position at all, and the sight sent a jab of irritation through me. That was the trouble with doing things this way. There wasn't the time to create the emotional connection with a person that made me more forgiving. If I cared, I could see past the not-so-pretty moments of their lives, but I couldn't care for someone I barely knew.

I nudged the back of his foot with mine. Our boots almost matched.

"Come on, up you get."

He complied, pushing himself back up. He didn't turn to look at me, but kept going, dragging himself through the dirt.

I exhaled a long sigh. This wasn't working. I wanted more.

"Okay, enough already. It's time now."

That gurgling whine came again, and he picked up his pace, fingers digging like claws into the dirt, as though he might somehow drag himself up the hill. Standing over him, I reached down and wrapped my fingers around the handle of the knife. I loved that connection, the sensation of being inside someone. This had never been sexual for me, not like that, but nothing was better than this feeling of power.

Locking my other arm around his head, I dragged the blade through his throat, opening him up. Blood spurted, soaking instantly into the ground, vanishing into the earth.

Ashes to ashes. Dust to dust.

There were many reasons a person could go missing in the Highlands. An accident—a fall from a cliff, perhaps. Or maybe they chose to vanish off the face of the earth, money or relationship problems driving them to it. Peat bogs could grab an unwary walker by the ankles and refuse to release them, dragging them deeper with each of the victim's struggles.

It didn't have to be murder.

The killing wasn't perfect. I preferred the buildup, the control over another person. This way, it was all over too quickly. But my days of making this last were over, weren't they? I'd come too close to getting caught, and if that happened, I wouldn't be able to do anything. I thought I might go mad in that situation. If I was unable to fulfil the need driving me, I might as well be dead.

It was done. No more life remained inside the man's body. I glanced around, wondering what to do with him now.

I spotted a small clump of gorse bushes off the beaten track. That would do. I grabbed him by the legs, right above where his walking boots met his ankles, and pulled.

Moving a body was backbreaking work. I'd always found it strange how a dead person weighed so much more than someone who was still alive. Scientifically, it shouldn't have made any difference.

The weight of the body dragging through the gorse had left a trail of broken stems, crushed leaves, and flowers. That displeased me. Though it was highly unlikely anyone would notice as they walked by, I still made the effort to go back over the track, using my foot to disturb the uniform layering of the crushed vegetation.

By the time the body was found, it would be weathered, nibbled by insects, maybe even larger animals. Weeks would have passed, possibly months, or longer. The fibres from my clothes were all popular brands that most walkers wore, I made sure of that, as were my gloves. There was the chance I'd left a strand of hair, but it most likely would have blown away by the time he was found. Besides, I knew from the evening spent in the pub that he was around plenty of other people who could easily have shed DNA over him. They may be brought in for questioning, if the police had their data on file, but they would soon be released.

My DNA *was* on file, but the police would have to do one thing before they could bring me in. One thing I had no intention of happening.

They would have to catch me.

Chapter One

G race Banks stared out of the window at the unfamiliar scenery passing by, her forehead pressed to the cool glass, the vibrations of the moving train running through her body.

Was she doing the right thing? It would be easy enough, once she'd reached the station, to simply jump on a returning train and head home. She could call up the tour company and tell them she'd been taken sick suddenly and could no longer make it. Surely, they wouldn't mind being one person short for the trip. It would be one less mouth to feed, one less person to look after.

She exhaled a long, shaky breath. No, she had promised herself she would go through with this, even if the thought sent her heart pattering, her chest tightening as though her ribs were compressing her lungs. It would do her good. It would be an escape from the stuffy house, and the memories, and the loneliness. All that space and fresh air would give her time to think. Actually, it wasn't *time* she was short of. It was the mental space. The clarity in her mind.

Grace had won the holiday after sharing a post from the hiking company on Facebook. She'd honestly thought those kinds of things were mostly a scam, but the photographs of the vast lochs, mountains, and glens had been beautiful enough for her to want to share anyway—the entry into the tour guide's giveaway had just been a bonus. She'd never actually expected to win.

Seven days of hill walking in the Cairngorms National Park in the Scottish Highlands.

What the hell was she thinking?

She felt as though she'd been on a train forever. She'd caught it first thing that morning from London to Aberdeen, where she'd changed for a connection to a smaller town with a Scottish name that she was never sure she was pronouncing correctly. She'd been promised door-to-door transfer by the company running the trip, but she was still nervous no one would show up to meet her at the station.

Though the stay and the walk itself was part of the package she'd won, she had needed to spend a small fortune on gear. Hiking wasn't something she'd ever done previous to this, and she didn't even own a pair of decent boots. She'd gone and got kitted out with full waterproofs, a day pack, thick socks and the walking boots. None of it had been cheap, but she reasoned with herself that the rest of the holiday was free. Besides, it wasn't as though she'd spent any money on herself for the last couple of years. Circumstances had meant she'd not been able to go anywhere, at least not for any length of time.

She'd lied to the organisers when she'd said she was an experienced hiker. They'd warned her that this trek didn't go by the usual trails and was intended for those with plenty of miles under their belt. Not only that, she'd also be carrying her one-person tent the whole way and would be expected to erect it each night and take it down again. From the research she'd done, many of these expeditions involved walking from one spot to another, but always staying in a proper accommodation.

Seemed she'd lucked out on that part, and they'd be wild camping instead. There weren't any buildings where they were going. The camping was all part of the experience. Getting to know her fellow hikers around a campfire, heating up cans of beans and roasting marshmallows. She hadn't had the guts to tell the organisers that aside from one trip with the Girl Guides at the age of eleven, she'd never even camped. Still, it couldn't be that hard, could it? She'd made sure she'd practised putting up and taking down the tent in the back garden several times already. The bloke she'd spoken to in the hiking shop had assured her that these tents were so easy, a child could do it. He probably wasn't wrong, but it hadn't been the putting up of the tent she'd struggled with the most, it had been getting it down again and back in its bag. Still, at twenty-four years old, she was young and physically fit. Maybe she should have got some extra walking practise in, but she was sure she'd be fine.

Grace glanced around at the people she shared the train carriage with. Were any of them heading the same way as her? She searched their faces for any signs that they might be walkers, but, in this situation, it was impossible to tell. A man in his sixties with a belly that stretched at an ugly jumper held a newspaper in front of his face, occasionally muttering and shaking his head at something he'd read. A mother with a blond-haired boy, of around three, sat staring out of the window while the boy was engrossed in playing on a tablet. A curly-haired young man in a shirt, the tie pulled loosely around his neck, his jacket thrown over the seat beside him, focused on his phone with the same kind of intensity that the three-year-old gave his game.

No, she didn't think any of them were planning any hiking trips. But then again, she doubted she looked the part either.

Or maybe she did. She was wearing the hiking boots she'd purchased at an exorbitant price, and the backpack was a brand known among walkers—or so the man in the hiking shop had told her—but she felt like she had 'novice' written in ink across her forehead.

Guilt washed over her at the thought of the house all locked up and empty. Would her mother know she'd left? Would she be angry? It was stupid, but the thought thickened her throat, and she blinked back tears. The distance had made her feel farther from her memories, and in a way, that felt like a betrayal.

A voice came over the tannoy, announcing the approaching station.

Grace's stomach flipped. After almost eight hours of travelling, she was finally here.

Before the train came to a halt, she got to her feet. The big rucksack that contained her equipment was on a rack nearer the door, and she wobbled her way between the two rows of seats towards it. She didn't trust herself to haul it onto her shoulders until the train had stopped fully, worried that if she lost her balance she'd end up sprawled on her back and unable to get up like a tortoise that had been flipped over.

She ducked down a little and scanned the platform as the train pulled into the station. Was it going to be easy to spot the people who were supposed to be picking her up? What if they'd forgotten, and she found herself stranded? No, it would be fine. She knew the name and address of where they were starting from, and she could easily jump in a taxi, assuming there were even taxis all the way out here.

A worry is like paying interest on a debt you never owe, her mother's voice sounded in her head.

The train came to a complete stop, and Grace reached out of the carriage window to open the door. Panic filled her at the possibility she wouldn't get the door open in time, and the train would continue with her still on board, taking her to some other remote part of Scotland she didn't know, but then the door swung open, and she clambered out, hanging on to her backpack.

She lifted her head, simultaneously searching for the exit and any sign that someone had come to meet her.

A woman, in her late twenties to early thirties, strode over. She was tall and incredibly thin, her blonde hair cut short in a wavy bob.

"Well, hallo there," the woman greeted her with a thick Scottish accent. "I'm guessing you're Grace."

"Yes, I am." Grace glanced around at the other people getting off the train. "How did you know?"

"You cannae be anyone else."

"Oh. Right." She didn't know what else to say to that.

"I'm Ainslie, from Wilderness Walking. The minibus is out in the car park."

Grace hadn't even managed to haul her bag onto her shoulders again, but Ainslie had already turned, her long legs quickly putting distance between her and Grace, who was still on the platform. The woman had made no offer to help with all of Grace's bags and equipment. Grace experienced a frisson of irritation but then tamped it down. She was supposed to be hiking with all this stuff, and if she couldn't even carry it from the train to the minibus, how the hell was she going to manage almost a week of hiking in the wilderness?

Bent against the weight on her back, she trailed after Ainslie to the car park. They headed for a white minivan with the name of the tour company emblazoned on the side. Ainslie had already opened the rear doors, and Grace joined her at the back. She let the heavy rucksack fall from her shoulders once more, and Ainslie reached out and took it from her.

Ainslie easily threw the rucksack with all the camping equipment strapped on top into the back. Though Ainslie was so thin Grace could make out the bones across her chest, her arms were sinewy with muscle, and she was clearly far stronger than Grace.

It was a beautiful day, the sky an endless stretch of blue, though there was a chill to the wind. Ainslie didn't seem to notice, however, and the goose bumps that popped up on Grace's skin were absent from Ainslie's, and she was only wearing a strappy vest top.

"How far is it to the house?" Grace asked as she climbed into the passenger seat. She'd considered getting in the back, but since there was only the two of them, it felt a bit weird.

Ainslie slid behind the wheel, pulled the door shut behind her, and started the engine. "About a thirty-minute drive. It's a pretty one, though."

"Thirty minutes is nothing compared to how far I've already come." She'd literally been travelling since daybreak.

Ainslie drove the minibus out of the car park and onto the road. "You've come up from London, is that right?"

"Yes."

"Bit different here, I bet."

"Very different," Grace agreed. "But different is good. I needed to get away."

She'd been expecting the other woman to dig deeper into her reasons for wanting to come so far from home all alone, but Ainslie simply nodded, as though she couldn't think of any reason for someone *not* to want to get away.

The town the train station served was tiny, more of a village than a town. They drove through the centre, which contained a corner shop, a butcher's, a bakery, a post office—all the individual establishments that had long been put out of business in the city by big supermarket chains.

"I was the only one on that train then?" she asked.

She was pointing out the obvious, but she didn't like the silence. There had been too much of it in her life lately. She was aware that it was ironic she was coming to one of the quietest and most desolate parts of the country in order to escape the silence of her London home. The silence wasn't caused by the constant traffic, or people, or alarms that seemed to go off at any time of night. It was in her head. A buzzing like static that fizzed up inside her, filling her brain and throwing adrenaline through her body in a flight or fight response, when she had no one to fight and nothing to run from.

"Aye, you were the only one on that train."

"So, are the others on the hike already here?"

Ainslie nodded, not taking her eyes off the winding road. They'd quickly left the buildings of the small town behind them. "A handful of them are. We're still waiting on some others."

"Will they be arriving on a different train?" Grace couldn't help feeling curious about the people she'd be on the walk with.

"One couple is driving down, I think."

"Oh, right."

A couple. She hoped they weren't all in couples. She didn't want to feel like a spare part.

Ainslie must have read her mind, and she looked away from the road to glance towards Grace. "Don't worry, it's not all couples. Plenty of single people, too. No' that it's like an eighteen-to-thirties kind of holiday, though. Our demographic tends to be older. Everyone's got the same kind of attitude."

Grace nodded. "Yes, of course."

She certainly wasn't there for any kind of hook-up. That was the last thing on her mind. Over the past few years, she'd had moments where she'd pondered on if it might be nice to have someone with her, to shoulder all the heartache, but she'd dismissed the idea just as quickly. Getting involved with someone would mean emotional investment, and she didn't have enough strength to give anything to anyone else. A relationship came with complications of its own—complications she could do without. Besides, where would she even have met someone? She was in the house twenty-four seven, especially after she'd had to give up work. It wasn't as though she could go out to bars and clubs when she was needed at home, and she didn't like the idea of meeting someone online. It all felt too seedy, swiping left or right on profiles as though they were a produce to procure instead of an actual human being. The thought of someone doing the same to her left her nauseated.

She leaned the side of her head against the passenger window, watching the world go by. The road was narrow and winding, hugging the curves of the hill as it climbed up into the Highlands.

They turned a bend, and Ainslie slammed on the brakes.

Grace straightened to discover a small flock of sheep, with thick, shaggy coats and twin curved horns on either side of their heads. A couple of good-sized lambs stuck close to their mother's side, but none of the animals seemed in any rush to move out of the way of the minivan.

Ainslie beeped the horn, but the sheep barely lifted their heads.

"This is what is known as rush hour out here," Ainslie joked.

She opened the driver's door and climbed out.

Grace stayed in her seat, unsure what was expected of her. Should she get out and help? She'd never been anywhere near sheep until now.

"Out the way, ye wee buggers," Ainslie shouted at the sheep, clapping her hands and then shooing them off the road. A couple of the sheep started, and that sent a ripple through the others, too.

Could sheep be dangerous? What would happen if one of them tried to butt Ainslie or something? Or was Grace thinking of goats? Her city upbringing was going to show her up if she wasn't careful.

With the sheep off the road, Ainslie climbed back behind the wheel and set off again.

"Do you get much wildlife up here?" Grace wished she'd done a little more research about that kind of thing.

"Oh, aye. We have deer, eagles, whales, bears—"

She stared at her. "Bears? You have bears?"

Ainslie managed to compose her expression for long enough to see the horror at the idea of camping in a tiny one-person tent in an area where bears roamed freely cross Grace's face, and then she crumpled in laughter.

"No, no bears. Sorry. I could no' resist."

Grace held her hand to her chest. "Thank God for that. I thought the sheep were bad enough."

Ainslie gave her a curious look. "So, where do you normally like to walk?"

Damn. She'd let her city girl show through too much. "Oh, umm, a few different places. I mean, there isn't a whole lot around London, so I always end up having to travel."

Grace wondered if they'd bothered to go through her Facebook page after she'd won the giveaway. Surely an experienced hiker would have plenty of photographs and tales about their excursions? But actually, other than a handful of old school friends, there wasn't much on hers at all. What could she have really posted about? The news she had wasn't the sort of thing people wanted to read about. She shared the occasional news story or a television show, or the post where she'd won this holiday, but she very rarely shared anything personal.

"Aye, whereabouts?" Ainslie wasn't going to give up.

Grace wanted to make something up, but chances were the spot she'd choose would be one of the other woman's favourites and she didn't want to get caught out in a lie.

She remembered that long-ago trip with the Girl Guides. "The last one was to the Brecon Beacons," she said, sticking to at least a part of the truth.

"I hear it's beautiful there."

"It is," she agreed. "Waterfalls and hills and mountains."

"Higher mountains in Scotland, though," Ainslie commented.

Grace got the sense Ainslie felt a little rivalry between Scotland and Wales.

"Yes. I think you're right."

They fell into silence for the rest of the journey. Fifteen minutes later, Ainslie slowed the minibus.

"Here we are," she declared.

She swung the vehicle through a gate that was already standing open. A low stone wall surrounded a pretty red-brick house which stood in the middle of the yard.

Grace's stomach flipped with fresh nerves.

Ainslie pulled the minibus to a stop and then opened the driver's door. She paused for a moment and looked back at Grace still sitting in the passenger seat. "Ready to meet some of the others?"

Grace forced a smile. "Ready as I'll ever be."

Chapter Two

Grace opened the passenger door and jumped down into the yard. The place appeared to have been stables at some point, or perhaps had once been used to farm some of the sheep like the ones they'd seen back on the road. The property was clearly now the headquarters for 'Wilderness Walkers' as it proudly said so on the side of the house.

Movement came from the front door, and a man around the same age as Ainslie walked out. He was attractive, with curly brown hair and a wide smile, and he lifted his hand in a wave.

"Welcome!" he called to them.

"This is my husband and business partner, Jack," Ainslie said. "We run Wilderness Walkers together."

"Good to meet ya." Jack stepped forward and shook Grace's hand.

Grace was surprised to hear an Australian accent, or perhaps it was a New Zealand one? She'd never quite managed to tell the difference between the two.

"You sound like you're a long way from home." Grace offered him a smile.

"Nah, this is home for me. It's been ten years now, hasn't it, babe?" He threw the final comment at Ainslie. "Can't see myself living anywhere else."

Grace nodded as though in agreement, but she couldn't imagine living up here permanently. She supposed there were plenty of people coming and going because of the business, and the town was only half an hour away, but what did they do outside of that? It wasn't as though they could pop to the cinema or head out shopping, or even order a takeaway when they didn't feel like cooking. And besides, even though it was absolutely gorgeous out here right now, when it was the start of summer and the sun was bright, she imagined it would be a whole different story during the winter. She couldn't imagine there would be much call for people to go on hiking tours in the freezing cold.

The two of them must really enjoy each other's company.

"I assume this is where we'll be spending the first night," she said.

Jack nodded. "That's right. You'll spend tonight here, then leave tomorrow morning, which is the Monday, then spend the week camping out in the wilderness. On the Saturday, I'll come and pick you guys up from our meeting spot. Then you'll have one night back in the house, and home again next Sunday."

"You'll be the one picking us up from our camping?" she checked.

She was surprised that Ainslie was the one who'd be leading the hike, instead of Jack. But then she shook the thought from her head. She shouldn't be so judgemental. Why wouldn't Ainslie do it, just because she was a woman?

"Jack handles most of the organisational side of things," Ainslie explained, as though picking up on Grace's thoughts. "He's good with all things to do with computers and advertising, like the social media campaigns." She flapped a hand in the air. "I can't be doing with all of that. Sitting in front of a computer for more than five minutes at a time is my idea of hell."

"Do most of your visitors camp?" she asked.

Ainslie shrugged. "Depends. We have enough bedrooms here to accommodate everyone. Some of those who prefer a more leisurely pace book in on holidays where they can return here for the night and have a home-cooked meal, but those of us who prefer to challenge ourselves a little more will only stay here for the first and final night."

Grace forced a smile and nodded, all the while wishing she'd asked if she could change her trip to the more leisurely kind.

"As I'm sure you read in your introduction email, we'll still be providing all your meals for you, so we'll get you kitted out with your food supplies before you set out in the morning."

Jack turned to glance over his shoulder, back towards the house. "Ah, here are some of the other walkers."

A couple who Grace guessed to be in their late thirties to early forties emerged from the front door. The woman's dark hair was cut in a cute pixie style, while her husband was short and skinny, his hair thinning on top. Grace thought he was batting above his weight, but then looks weren't everything.

"This is Craig and Isla," Jack said. "They're returning to us for the third year in a row. Guys, this is Grace."

Both the man and woman lifted a hand in a wave and said 'hi.'

Isla nudged her husband in the ribs. "Apologies in advance for his snoring, though. Canvas walls don't do much for noise control."

"It's not a snore, it's more like a purr," he retorted good-naturedly.

Jack stepped in. "Everyone's so exhausted by the time they get their heads down, no one hears a thing anyway."

Grace liked the sound of that. A good night's sleep was something that had evaded her for a long time now. She couldn't remember the last time she'd gone to bed and fallen asleep without tossing and turning for at least a couple of hours beforehand. And then, when she did eventually fall asleep, she woke at the slightest sound, as though her body was primed for it. She knew the reason why, but she should have been able to shake the habit by now.

A younger man appeared in the doorway behind them. Someone who was closer to her age, she thought.

"Hi, I'm Scott. Good to see I'm not the only one on my own."

She hoped he didn't think she was fair game.

"Oh, you're not," Ainslie stepped in. "There's someone else coming alone as well, though they're not here yet."

"Male or female?" Grace asked, hoping she was going to say female.

"Male." She must have seen Grace's expression. "Sorry, but don't worry, you've always got me." She threw Grace a wink.

Grace relaxed a fraction.

"Hey, and me," Isla protested. "I want to get to join in on the girl talk, too."

Grace found herself smiling. "Absolutely."

Could she make some friends on this trip? She hadn't been so sure earlier, but now she was thinking it would actually be fun to spend time with these women. They were a little older than her, but that didn't matter, did it? They were all still adults.

A grumble of an engine approaching from the road drew everyone's attention, the conversation dying away. Tyres crunched on gravel, and an old grey Range Rover pulled in through the gates.

"Looks like we have another arrival," Jack announced.

The Range Rover drew to a halt, and the passenger and driver's doors opened simultaneously. A man in his fifties climbed out of the driver's side, and a red-haired woman of a similar age got out of the passenger side and rounded the vehicle. The woman smiled self-consciously, while the man threw the waiting crowd a wide grin and then stomped on over with his hand held out.

"Dinnae think we were going to make it," the man declared, his Scottish accent thick. "But we got here!"

Jack and Ainslie stepped forward to meet them.

The man gave Jack a wide smile and clapped him on the back as though they'd known each other forever. She guessed this was another couple who were returning here after coming on previous years.

"How ye doin'?'" The man's dark hair was streaked with grey, his face weathered with deep lines across his forehead. "I'm Fraser Donnel."

"I'm good, thanks, mate," Jack said. "I'm Jack, and I'm one of the people who runs things up here." He gestured to his wife. "This lovely lady is Ainslie. She's the one who'll be doing the hike with you guys."

"Good to meet you, Ainslie," Fraser said.

He looked over his shoulder to where the woman had followed him from the car. "This here is Nicola."

The woman smiled. She seemed a little overwhelmed by her outgoing husband.

"This is Grace." Jack introduced her to the new arrivals. "She'll be joining us on the walk. And over here we have Scott, Craig, and Isla."

"Hi," Grace said to Fraser. "It's good to meet you."

The Scotsman frowned at her, as though trying to pin her accent. "You sound like you've come a lot farther than we have."

"Yes," she agreed. "I travelled up from London today."

He pulled a face. "Rather you than me."

She laughed. "Thanks."

Grace turned her attention to Nicola, who'd so far been standing back from the introductions. The other woman had an expensive-looking camera hanging around her neck. Grace guessed she had an interest in photography.

"Hi," she said. "I'm Grace."

The woman smiled, lighting up her face. With her red hair and pale skin, she really was quite beautiful. Grace could see what Fraser saw in her. Even though Fraser was clearly far older than her, he was still an attractive man, too.

"Nice to meet you."

Despite Nicola's Celtic appearance, to Grace's relief, she detected an English accent. She'd been a little worried she wouldn't understand everything Fraser was saying, but at least his wife would be there to translate, if needed.

"So, we're just waiting on one more," Ainslie said, "but he did warn us he might not be here until either late or first thing, so I suggest we get on with things without him. We'll show you all to your rooms, and then dinner will be in about an hour, if that's okay with everyone. If you need drinks or something sooner, give us a shout."

Ainslie led them into the house and then showed Grace up the stairs. They were narrow, and Grace worried she was going to get her backpack stuck in the stairwell, but she managed to get through without a problem. Did it make it easier for those hiking in couples, she wondered? Would the women be carrying as much as she was, or would their husbands carry some of it for them?

"This is your room for the night." Ainslie stopped in front of a stripped wooden door at the end of the hallway. "It's only small, I'm afraid, but since I'm sure you're used to staying in a tent, it'll feel like luxury."

Grace forced a smile. Yeah, she was only used to staying in a tent if staying in one over ten years ago counted. "I'm sure it'll be fine."

The room was basic but seemed comfortable enough. The square window had a deep sill, displaying the thickness of the walls of the house. The wooden floor was covered in a woven rug, and a dressing table and a set of drawers were pushed up against the far wall. There was no wardrobe, but Grace guessed the people who stayed here most likely wouldn't be bringing the kinds of clothes where they'd worry about them getting creased.

"The bathroom is right down the hall, last door you come to. You might want to watch the hot and cold in the shower, though. One tiny turn and you can go from arctic to scalding."

Grace smiled. "Thanks for the warning."

"Enjoy it. No showers when we're out in the wild, right?"

"No, I guess not."

She'd brought a packet of baby wipes, and the introductory email had talked about bringing swimwear for dips in the ice-cold lochs. She wasn't sure she liked the sound of that either, but she might be grateful for the wash after several days hiking with no running water.

"Right, well, I'll leave you to get settled in. Our room is the small extension behind the kitchen. Come and knock if you need anything."

"I will, thanks."

Ainslie gave her a final smile and left, closing the door behind her.

Grace dropped her backpack onto the floor and then plonked onto the edge of the bed. She looked around the compact room, wondering what to do with herself for the next hour. There was no point in unpacking, since she was going to be taking everything with her tomorrow. She sucked in a steadying breath. She hoped she was going to be able to keep up with everyone. The last thing she wanted was to make a show of herself.

The thought of a shower sounded good. She was tired and sticky from travelling all day and could use a freshen-up and a change of clothes before dinner.

She had a microfibre towel the man in the hiking shop had sold her. It was ridiculously thin and didn't look as though it would be much good at all—definitely not like her usual big fluffy bath sheets—but he'd insisted this was what everyone used, and that there was no way she'd be able to fit a normal towel into her pack. He had a point. It was very light and rolled up tightly, and she would be grateful not to have the extra weight after she'd walked for twenty miles.

Not wanting to be tiptoeing down the hallway with only the thin towel wrapped around her, she opened her pack to locate a change of clothing, as well as her washbag. Aware that it was a shared bathroom, she'd have to make sure she showered and changed quickly so she didn't keep people waiting.

Taking her stuff with her, she slipped out of the bedroom and hurried towards the bathroom. The door was already open a crack, and as she reached for the handle, the door opened.

The younger man who was also here on his own appeared on the other side. He was naked apart from a towel similar to her own wrapped around his hips.

"Oh, sorry." She apologised automatically, even though she hadn't done anything to apologise for. Such a British thing to do. She wondered if the Scots were a little more brusque.

"No problem." He flashed her a wide grin and raised his eyebrows in a question. "See you down at dinner?"

Her cheeks heated. She racked her mind for his name. Scott. That was it. "Yes, see you down there."

He brushed past, and she stepped into the bathroom and shut the door behind her. It was stupid that she let herself get flustered just because of the close proximity of a stranger.

How was she going to manage when she only had a bit of canvas between her and the outside world?

Chapter Three

By the time she made it downstairs, feeling better after her shower and a quick change of clothes, most of the guests were already sitting around the long dining room table.

Grace scanned the chairs, trying to spot an empty one.

Several faces turned towards her, but she didn't see Ainslie or Jack among them. The two of them were most likely busy making dinner for all their guests. There was a spare seat next to Scott, but she didn't want to give him any ideas, especially after catching him in only a towel. There was also an empty spot next to the female half of the younger couple, Isla, and so Grace rounded the table and paused behind the chair.

"Is this okay?" she asked, still nervous. So much time had passed since she'd spent time with people socially, she was sure she was going to make some faux pas that people would be talking about behind her back.

Isla shifted her seat back slightly and motioned Grace into the empty spot. "Yes, please. Come join us."

She sank gratefully into the chair.

"Are you all ready for tomorrow?" Isla asked.

"As I'll ever be."

"Have you done much of this kind of thing?"

"Oh, some," she said, deliberately being vague. She knew there were going to be a lot of conversation around walking, but she hadn't realised everyone was going to start with it. She wished she'd actually got some proper practise in, if only so she had something to talk about. "I live in London, and it's not been easy getting away recently. I loved it up on the Brecon Beacons when I was there last time, though," she said, rehashing what she'd said to Ainslie in the minivan.

"Yes, it is beautiful there," Isla agreed. "I love all the waterfalls."

"Yes, me, too." She tried to remember what her twelve-year-old brain had stored away about the place at the time. She glanced over at Isla's husband. "Do you and your husband walk together often? It must be lovely to have shared interests."

She wanted to get the conversation away from herself.

"Yes, it is." Isla raised her voice slightly and threw an elbow into her husband's ribs. "Isn't that right, Craig?"

Craig had been talking about something with Fraser on his other side, and he turned and smiled, though Grace got the feeling the smile wasn't completely genuine. "I'm sorry, what?"

"I was just saying to Grace how great it is that we have shared interests."

Was it her imagination, or did Isla seemed to be trying too hard? She picked up on a little tension between the couple, and it was making Grace uncomfortable. She looked around hoping to join in on someone else's conversation but discovered Scott staring at her from the other side of the table. She caught his eye and had no choice but to smile back so she didn't appear rude.

"I'm sorry about earlier," he said, his forearms on the table-top as he leaned across slightly to be heard. "I didn't mean to embarrass you."

She flapped a hand, trying to dismiss his comment. "Oh, you didn't, honestly. I was fine."

"No, it was my fault. I should have considered that not all women want to be greeted with a specimen of male perfection when they haven't first prepared themselves for it."

Male perfection? Was he joking? Admittedly, he was attractive, and from what she'd seen, he was in perfectly good shape, but surely people didn't actually talk about themselves like that. There wasn't any kind of a smile on his face, and he hadn't laughed. She had no idea what her reaction was supposed to be.

Movement came from the direction of the kitchen, and she was relieved when Ainslie and Jack entered, both holding steaming plates of food.

"Here we go, guys," Jack said. "Sorry to keep you all waiting, but I hope it'll be worth it."

Jack placed a bowl of beef stew in gravy with creamy mashed potato in front of her. Separate dishes of vegetables were brought out and set on the table. It was the start of summer, and at home she'd have been eating salads or fish, but somehow this meal felt appropriate.

"You're lucky to have such a good cook as a wife," Craig commented to Jack.

Ainslie laughed. "I don't think so. I can burn water. Jack's the cook around here."

Jack nodded and grinned. "It's true. I do all the cooking."

"Seriously?" Craig lifted his glass in Jack's direction. "You're full of surprises. And there was me thinking the Aussie's only knew how to cook if it was on a barbecue."

Isla jabbed her husband in the ribs again and shot him a glare. Was she trying to stop him going down the route of stereotypical insults? To Grace it had only sounded like good-natured banter.

Grace took a big mouthful of food, the aroma of the meat and gravy suddenly making her realise how hungry she was. It really was delicious—the meat falling apart, the vegetables tender, but still with bite.

"Hang on," Scott spoke up. "If Ainslie is leading the hike, and Jack is staying here, does that mean Ainslie will be in charge of the cooking while we're away?"

Ainslie grinned. "Aye, sorry, though you're all welcome to take it in turns. It's all part of the experience."

"The experience of giving everyone food poisoning, if you're having to eat my cooking," Fraser threw in.

Everyone laughed.

Grace hoped he was joking. The possibility of having food poisoning while out in the middle of nowhere was not a pleasant thought.

She noted how quiet Fraser's wife had been. She'd barely said a word over dinner but had smiled and chuckled with the rest of them. It couldn't be easy to be in a relationship with someone like Fraser. It wasn't that he was particularly physically big, but something about his nature seemed to fill a room. Maybe Nicola was happy with the dynamic that way. Opposites attracted. If she was more of an introvert, perhaps having a very extroverted partner took some of the pressure away from her having to get more involved.

At least with all the big personalities around the table, it meant no one was looking too closely at Grace, either. She'd been worried they'd want to get her talking about her reasons for being here and poking into her life back in London, but so far, no one had really asked. It most likely wouldn't stay that way—especially when they'd be covering miles and miles with nothing but each other around them—but she was enjoying the anonymity for the moment.

Ainslie hovered around the table, making sure everyone's drinks were topped up. Grace stuck to water, though she eyed up the wine bottle wistfully. It wouldn't do her any good to have a hangover tomorrow, though she noticed a couple of the others, including Scott, weren't holding back.

"Aren't you joining us?" Grace asked their hostess.

Ainslie was the closest to her in age, and she was relieved the other woman was going to be coming on the hike as well.

"Nah, I've got too much to do. I'll let you all get to know each other."

Grace glanced at the empty chair, and then remembered.

Of course, they were still missing someone. Another guest would join them either later tonight or first thing in the morning, before they set off. Everyone else seemed friendly, and she hoped the new person wouldn't do anything to change the dynamics.

They finished eating, and everyone wandered off, some going through to the living room to continue their drinks. Even though she was a guest, Grace was painfully aware that she hadn't actually paid for any of this, and so she picked up some of the dirty plates and carried them through to the kitchen where Jack and Ainslie were washing up.

"You dinnae need to do that," Ainslie told her, accepting the dishes. "That's our job. Go and get to know your fellow walkers better."

"Oh, I don't mind."

"Well, we do," Jack said. "You're supposed to be on holiday."

Grace smiled, and turned and went back to the dining room.

She stopped in the doorway. Craig and Isla were both standing in the corner, and from their body language, they didn't appear to be enjoying each other's company. From her position, Grace couldn't help overhearing.

"What was that all about?" Isla hissed. "Implying that I can't even cook."

Craig wrinkled his nose in derision and shook his head. "What the fuck are you talking about?"

"I heard your tone—telling Jack he was lucky. It makes it sound as though you're not."

He folded his arms across his chest and raised both eyebrows. "Well, am I lucky, Isla? Am I really?"

She glared at him. "You promised you wouldn't do this!"

Craig rolled his eyes. "Oh, give me a break."

Grace stepped back from the doorway, feeling bad at having listened in on their conversation. She collided with a solid body and spun around. For a moment, she was sure she'd find herself face to face with Scott, but it was Fraser.

"Whoa there, lass." He held up both hands. "Everything all right?"

The voices from the other room had gone quiet. Did they know they'd been overheard?

"Yes, fine. I was just helping tidy up."

"You should get your rest. Might be the last chance for a while."

He threw her a wink and then turned and walked away, leaving Grace to slink off to bed. She hoped Craig and Isla hadn't figured out she'd eavesdropped on their fight. One thing was clear—the couple's seemingly perfect relationship wasn't so perfect after all.

Chapter Four

G race was awake early.

It had been the first night she hadn't spent in her own bed for as long as she could remember, and she'd lain awake for more than an hour before eventually falling asleep, and then had woken multiple times. How the hell was she going to manage to sleep at all when she was going to be sleeping on the ground, with nothing but a blow-up pillow, a sleeping bag, and a bit of canvas around her?

There's still time to drop out, her mother's voice chirped in her head. *Tell them you're not feeling well and need to go home.*

But the thought of going back to that cold, empty house was even worse than the idea of sleeping in a tent for the next five nights.

She'd been dying for a wee for the last couple of hours but hadn't wanted to make the trip down the hallway in the dark. The idea of bumping into Scott coming out of the bathroom again was enough to make her cross her legs, but she was going to need to get over it. Her bathroom for the next week was most likely going to consist of a bush.

Grace got up and dressed in the comfortable clothes and walking boots, and then nipped to the bathroom to relieve herself and brush her teeth. Movement and voices came from behind the doors of the other rooms she passed but thankfully she didn't bump into a half-naked Scott again.

She packed everything back into her pack and hauled it onto her shoulders to take downstairs. They were going to be leaving straight after breakfast and had been instructed to leave the bags by the front door to be loaded into the minivan. Jack would drive them all to their initial location and drop them off, and he'd be back for them in five days to pick them up again.

In the dining room, the breakfast had been laid out as a buffet—yogurt, muesli, oat cakes, hot porridge to be scooped out of a large pot with a ladle, boiled eggs, slices of black pudding and bacon. To drink, there was the choice of orange juice, tea, or coffee.

Several people were already up. She spotted Fraser and Nicola tucking in, and Scott was sitting with Craig, though it didn't appear as though Isla was down yet. Her thoughts went to the argument she'd overheard, and she wondered if they weren't talking. She hoped there wouldn't be tension between the two of them.

"Morning," Ainslie greeted upon seeing her. "Sleep well?"

"Yes, fine, thanks."

It was a lie, but she hadn't wanted to seem rude or insult them by saying that she hadn't. Her lack of sleep had nothing to do with the room or bed, and everything to do with her.

Jack joined them, carrying out a rack of fresh, hot toast. "Help yourself to breakfast," he told her. "Sorry it's only a buffet. I'll make sure there's a full Scottish breakfast for you all when you get back, but we need to get out early this morning, so this will have to do."

Grace couldn't see anything to apologise for. "Looks great to me."

"Get the calories into you," Ainslie said. "You're going to need them for what's ahead."

Ainslie didn't look as though she consumed any calories at all, but Grace watched as she piled her plate high with food. Ainslie somehow managed to both eat and walk the room at the same time, and Grace realised that the only occasion she'd seen the other woman sitting down was when she'd been driving the minibus. The boundless energy that radiated from her clearly contributed to her figure as well. Grace wished there was a way she could somehow siphon it from Ainslie for herself. She could certainly do with some this morning, especially after the bad night's sleep.

It wasn't as though she was paying for any of this food either. She felt a little guilty about the fact, but she guessed they got what they needed from the extra promo of the giveaway.

The others had noticed her arrival and called 'good morning' to her, giving her a smile or nod. Grace helped herself to toast, and bacon and eggs, but skipped the black pudding. It was still a little early for her to contemplate eating something that involved blood, fat, and suet. She poured herself a cup of strong tea as well and found a seat.

Isla entered the room and went straight to her husband and planted a kiss on his cheek. She was all smiles, so Grace assumed they'd made up again.

Grace felt better after she'd had something to eat—stronger and more able to cope with the idea of walking for the rest of the day. She got to her feet and picked up her plate, and some of the other empty dishes, and carried them back to the kitchen.

Scott was crouching at one of the cupboards, and he jolted away, hiding something beneath the bottom of his jumper.

"Oh, hi." He rose to his feet. "Everything all right?"

"Yes, fine." She slid the plates onto the side next to the sink. "What are you up to?"

He flashed her a wide smile. "Nothing much."

"You don't have to do that," Ainslie said as she entered the kitchen as well, nodding at the stack of dirty dishes. "Neither of you. You're supposed to be on holiday, remember?"

Had Scott been tidying away the plates as well? That was clearly what Ainslie had thought, though to Grace it looked as though Scott was searching for something. He'd certainly jumped when she'd walked into the kitchen, and what had he been hiding?

Unwilling to challenge him directly—it wasn't really any of her business—she went back out to where everyone else was still loitering.

"G'day, folks." Jack clapped once. "If everyone's done eating, we should get on the road. Your bags have already been loaded into the minibus, so it's just yourselves we need."

The energy in the room increased, everyone talking louder, clapping each other on the backs and laughing. She still felt on the outside of things, as though she wasn't quite one of them—which she wasn't—but their enthusiasm was rubbing off, and she suddenly found herself thinking this could be exciting. She had *wanted* to do this trip. No one had forced her into it. She'd known that she needed to do something different to break herself out of her rut, and just going to a hotel somewhere for a week wasn't going to do it. She'd needed something that would push her, and change her, and make her see that there was a different way to live.

Everyone gathered their belongings and piled towards the front of the house.

Ainslie handed each of the walkers their food supplies for the week. "Your lunch for today is included, together with all your dried supplies for the week. You're expected to carry your own water as well, though I have purifying tablets for when we need to refill."

Grace accepted her food package gratefully and added it to her pack, and then filed out after the others. The day was bright, though there was a nip to the air. It would most likely warm up later.

As she headed towards the minibus, she realised they weren't alone.

An older man, who she took to be in his early fifties, was already sitting in the back. So, this must be the mysterious additional walker who'd only arrived this morning. In all the excitement, she'd forgotten about him.

"Everyone, this is Malcolm," Jack said. "Malcolm, this is everyone. I'll let them introduce themselves, or we'll be here all day."

Grace gave Malcolm what she hoped was a welcoming smile—it must be hard joining when everyone had already started to get to know each other—but the older man's lips tightened, his cheeks barely flexing, and then he turned away again to stare out of the window.

Malcolm looked like he was going to be a laugh a minute.

She caught Isla's eye, and the other woman pulled a face. Grace was relieved to see she wasn't the only one who'd noticed the new arrival's less than friendly manner. She guessed it wasn't right to expect people to automatically be friendly or make an effort. A lot of people must do these walks to get away from others and all their social expectations, and he didn't owe any of them his friendship.

"It's only a twenty-minute drive to our starting point," Ainslie said, twisting around in her seat. "We'll cover about eight miles across the Highlands before we stop for lunch, and then the same again after lunch to where we'll stop for the night."

The minivan climbed higher, Grace watching the scenery pass by the window. It was beautiful out here, and they hadn't even started walking yet. They hadn't passed any other cars, and she hadn't even spotted any other walkers. All she saw were more sheep and some birds. An eagle circled lazily on some eddies, surveying the ground below for any small rodents for breakfast.

"Here we are." Jack pulled into a spot off the side of the road.

Grace had no idea why they'd chosen this as a starting point rather than anywhere else. It all looked very similar to her—all rolling hills, valleys, and winding roads.

Jack hooked his arm around his wife's waist and kissed her firmly on the mouth. "I'll see you on Saturday. Stay safe."

"I will." She gave him another quick kiss.

Grace glanced away, embarrassed, as though she'd intruded on a private moment.

"Everyone ready?" Ainslie turned back towards the group. "It's a perfect day for walking, but stay hydrated. We might be in Scotland, but the sun can still get hot. We should cover sixteen miles by the end of today." She must have caught sight of Grace's expression. "Think of all those lovely wee endorphins," Ainslie said with a grin, strapping on a backpack even bigger than Grace's.

The woman was far tougher than Grace would ever be.

Grace sucked in a breath and mentally steeled herself. She could do this. She was young and healthy, and it was only walking, after all. How hard could it be?

They set off, most people lifting their hands in a wave to Jack, who beeped the horn of the minibus as a farewell. The start of the trail led uphill. The group quickly separated, with the fastest and strongest striding to the front, and the others hanging back a little. Despite his age, the new arrival, Malcolm, paced on ahead, with Ainslie hot on his tail. Scott was close behind them, then Craig and Isla, while Grace hung back with Fraser and Nicola. Fraser was talking loudly in his strong accent but soon grew puffed and had to slow down, while Nicola seemed to good-naturedly put up with him. It wasn't that Fraser was a particularly big man, or even overweight. He was just stocky, in the way men of that age often were. A few too many whiskies or pints of ale most likely hadn't helped.

She studied the body language of Craig and Isla as they walked, too, though it was hard to tell what anyone was doing when they just looked like giant backpacks with legs sticking out of the bottom. Craig bumped his wife with his hip, and she playfully smacked his shoulder in return. They seemed happy enough. Perhaps this was where they worked best together, out here in the open, putting themselves through a physical challenge.

Her thighs ached by the time they reached the top of the hill, but she quickly forgot about the discomfort. The view beyond stole her breath. The highland dipped in a sweeping curve of green dotted in pink and purple heather, to the sparkling view of a loch beneath them.

"Wow. That's stunning," she blurted.

Scott was standing beside her. "Yeah, it certainly is."

"This is just the start," Isla said. "Wait until we get even more remote."

More remote? Was it possible to get any more remote? It wasn't as though there was a single house or even a road within sight.

"The other side of the loch will be our lunch break," Ainslie told them, her hands on her hips.

Lunch break, already? Grace slid her phone out of her pocket to check the time. Yes, they'd been walking well over an hour.

She used her phone to take a couple of photographs but was mindful of the battery. It wasn't as though there was anywhere to charge it up here. There wasn't any mobile phone reception, and it wasn't as though she had anyone to phone, but she didn't want to run out of charge and miss capturing any of the amazing shots of scenery she was sure she would get. Not that she was much of a photographer. She hadn't really had time in her life to figure out what it was she *was* good at.

Nicola used her expensive camera to take some photographs as well, and Grace made a mental note to have a chat with the other woman about what kind of equipment she would need to get started with some kind of proper photography. She hadn't seen a mobile phone anywhere near Nicola's hand, so she bet the other woman scoffed at the sort of photos Grace was managing to take.

Her earlier thought about lunchtime having arrived quickly soon died away once they started the descent to the loch. It was much farther than it had appeared from the top of the hill. Another hour had passed by the time they reached the water, and then they had to traverse the edge to the spot where Ainslie planned for them to stop for lunch.

Despite the huge pack Ainslie carried, their guide seemed as full of energy as she had when they'd set off. By contrast, every part of Grace's body was aching. The backpack pulled on her shoulders and made her lower back ache, and her thighs were trembling with exertion. Twinges in her calves threatened to cramp, and she was realising just how unfit she actually was. She hoped none of the others had noticed. Even the ones who were several decades older than her didn't seem to be struggling in the same way. But, she had to admit, despite the aching muscles, she was enjoying herself. She never would have got to experience all this untouched, natural beauty if she hadn't pushed herself to do this. She still wasn't completely sure about a couple of her fellow walkers, but everyone else seemed nice enough. They probably weren't all going to be friends for life, but she imagined they might send Facebook friend requests and maybe tag each other in some pictures. She'd suggest Instagram to them, but she didn't think many people over the age of thirty used it. Then again, what did she know?

"Everyone hungry?" Ainslie asked, drawing to a halt and dropping her pack down.

The group made affirmative comments and plonked both their bags and themselves onto the ground. There was plenty of groaning, and everyone stretched out stiff backs and legs. That was good. Grace wasn't the only one who was finding it a physical strain.

Grace was starving. She couldn't remember ever being so hungry. Her appetite hadn't been great recently, and sometimes she'd go the whole day and realised she'd forgotten to eat lunch. After the huge breakfast, she was surprised she wanted to eat again, but she definitely did.

She sat down and pulled the packed lunch Ainslie had given her out of her bag. They'd been asked for their preferences in the introductory email and had needed to tick if they'd wanted tuna or cheese. Grace had chosen tuna. It was in a wrap—more space-saving than regular bread—and with it was a small packet of trail mix and a chocolate-covered flapjack.

They were on a plateau beside the loch. The day was warm but not stiflingly so. Sun sparkled off the water, the surrounding mountains reflected in the glasslike surface.

An insect whined around her head, and Grace flapped her hand at it.

"Be happy we're not later in the summer," Ainslie commented. "Those things can make a walker's life absolute hell."

Grace slapped at one near her ear. "I can imagine."

"She's no' joking. Sometimes, there's so many, it's like you're walking through clouds of them," Fraser agreed.

Silence settled over the group as they all tucked into their lunch. Grace devoured her food. Had anything so simple ever tasted so good? She ate every scrap and was already looking forward to dinnertime, even if it was only going to be something either boiled up or rehydrated. The night-time, however, was a different story. She was worried she wouldn't be able to sleep being in a tent, surrounded by people she barely knew.

"What brings you out here, then?" Fraser asked her. His arms were wrapped around his shins, and he leaned forwards to look at her sitting on the other side of Nicola. "You don't seem like the usual kind of walker we get, at least not one who comes on her own."

Grace shrugged, trying to act nonchalant. She really didn't want to get into all the details right now. It was such a beautiful day, and she didn't want to drag either herself or anyone else down with the truth.

"Oh, you know. Stuff. I got sick of all the London bullshit. Everyone just wants to party or work. It felt like I should be doing something different. Something real."

"So, you booked this as a holiday?"

"Seemed better than going to Marbella and spending a week drunk on a beach, surrounded by other Brits."

He cocked an eyebrow. "That sounds like an ideal holiday for someone your age."

"Not for me."

"I guess not." He gestured around. "Well, you're here, aren't you?"

"Unless this is all some crazy hallucination."

He chuckled at that, and she was pleased she could make him laugh. At least he hadn't dug too deeply about what she'd been doing back in London, though they were only on their first day, and she was sure it would come up.

They rested a little longer and then got moving again, first making sure they'd picked up after themselves.

"The only thing we leave behind are our footsteps," Ainslie said.

If only life was like that all the time, Grace thought. It would be far less messy if people didn't leave anything behind after they'd gone. No broken-hearted relatives, no unpaid bills, no wardrobes filled with clothes they'd never wear or shelves of books they'd never read.

It would make the whole process a whole lot less painful.

Chapter Five

They walked for the rest of the afternoon.

From the loch, they took a narrow forest trail, the trees of pine, oak, and birch offering shade from the late sun. Grace was grateful for it. Within a couple of hours, she found herself struggling. The distance between herself and the rest of the group increased with every passing minute. Before long, the leading group of Ainslie, Craig and Isla, were so far ahead, that Grace lost sight of them. Malcolm came next, and Fraser and Nicola were right ahead of her. Though she hated being at the back, and was trying to get her legs to move fast enough to keep up with everyone else, she noticed Scott slowing with her. He glanced over his shoulder at her, offering her the occasional thumbs up to check she was okay. He'd been leading the group for most of that morning, and she knew he was only lagging because of her. She didn't want him to think she was an easy target, just because she was on her own.

They emerged from between the trees. The shapes of the mountains were printed against the horizon, but, for the moment at least, they were on another plateau.

Everyone had stopped, and Grace hoped they weren't all waiting for her, but then Ainslie took off her backpack and dropped it to the ground.

"This is where we're going to be spending the night, everyone. So, let's get our tents up while we've still got some daylight."

Grace hadn't noticed the waning of the sun while it had been hidden from view by the canopy of branches, but the light had definitely faded.

She was too tired to put up her tent, but she had no choice. She had to force her arms and legs to behave and do what was needed or she wasn't going to have anywhere to sleep tonight. As much as lying, looking up at the stars might sound romantic, in real life, it was just plain scary. She wasn't going to start asking any of the men to help her either. She might be young, but she was independent, and she hadn't relied on a man since her dad had walked out on them when she'd been a teenager.

She prayed she'd practised enough to make the job a simple one, and that she wasn't going to do something to make a mess of it. Knowing her luck, she'd have left one of the poles at home.

Selecting a spot that was a reasonable distance from everyone else, without being too far from them either, she checked the area for any rocks that would make sleeping uncomfortable and might damage the tent, and then emptied the contents of the storage bag out onto the ground. She spread out the protective sheet, and then laid out the inside of the tent. She put the poles together, to create two longer ones, which would cross over in the middle and provide the base for the inside of the tent to attach to, and then the top layer of the tent would go over that. The bloke in the camping store had told her the different names for each of the layers, but she'd long since forgotten them.

When she was done, she threw her backpack inside and then laid out her sleeping mat and sleeping bag. There was no room to stand inside the tent, but it looked cosy enough. If only she had an actual bed, though. Her back already ached from carrying the backpack for miles. How the hell was she going to feel in the morning after a night basically sleeping on the ground?

Her stomach gurgled, asking when it was dinnertime. She crawled back out of the tent to see everyone else was already done and were now sitting in the small clearing they'd naturally created with the positions of their tents.

"We're having the macaroni and cheese tonight, everyone," Ainslie announced to the group. "It's easier if we all try to stick to the same meals so we can cook up a big batch rather than having lots of individual pots to clean."

Grace was happy with that. She'd never have dreamed of eating rehydrated macaroni and cheese in her normal life, but here it was all about plenty of carbs and calories.

One thing she discovered about this type of cooking was that it was fast, and within fifteen minutes she found herself holding a bowl of steaming hot pasta. She barely tasted it; the only thing holding her back from devouring it as quickly as she had the tuna wrap at lunchtime was her fear of burning her mouth.

Once everyone had finished eating, some people wandered off to their tents, while others stayed sitting where they'd eaten.

Ainslie produced a treat of marshmallows and dark chocolate, which they melted on top of digestive biscuits. Again, this wasn't something Grace would normally eat, but it was delicious, and she appreciated the sugar rush.

A couple of the group didn't join in. Malcolm had disappeared to his tent as soon as they'd finished eating, and Scott climbed back inside his, as well. It wasn't dark just yet, but she imagined the moment the sun slipped behind the hills, they'd all end up going to bed.

Scott resurfaced from his tent and took a seat next to Isla. Craig had vanished behind the trees—most likely needing to relieve himself—and within moment Scott and Isla were laughing together.

She turned to talk to Fraser and Nicola again.

Movement and a yell of surprise caught Grace's attention, and she whipped her head back around. Craig was standing behind Isla and had grabbed her arm. He dragged her to her feet and pulled her away, past the small circle of tents, and then kept walking.

An awkward silence fell over the group. Grace didn't know if she should keep an eye on what was happening or if she should stare at the ground and give them their privacy.

Craig had been overly rough with Isla. What was he angry with her for? Just talking to Scott? Or was it about something else? They'd been arguing the previous night, too. Besides, Isla hadn't been doing anything wrong. Just because she was married didn't mean she wasn't allowed to talk to another man.

Craig had pulled Isla out of earshot, but it was easy to see they were still fighting. Craig was leaning in towards his wife, his finger jabbed in her face. Isla threw her hands in the air and then spun away from him, but he seized hold of her arm again and yanked her back.

Grace shot Ainslie a concerned look. "Should we do something?"

Ainslie frowned and bit her lip. "I'm not sure..."

Craig shoved his wife backwards, and Isla fell on the ground.

"Hey!"

Movement came from beside Grace, and Fraser was suddenly on his feet, moving surprisingly fast for a man in his fifties. He ran past Ainslie and got in between Isla and Craig. He turned his back to Craig and helped Isla to her feet. Ainslie had gone after him, and when she reached them she immediately went to Isla, taking her hand and guiding her away from Craig.

The timbre of Fraser's deep Scottish tone carried over to the group in a way Craig's voice hadn't. "You dinnae lay your hands on a woman, pal! What the hell is wrong with ye?"

"It's okay, Fraser, just leave it," Isla called over to him.

"It's none of your business," Craig spat back.

"If you think we're gonnae stand by while you treat her like that, you can think again."

Craig pointed at Isla. "How about how she treats me? I guess no one cares about that, do they?"

"Please, Craig," Isla begged. "Just leave it."

Craig gave a growl of frustration and stormed away from them. Without saying another word, he climbed inside the tent he shared with Isla.

Isla threw them all an apologetic look. "I'm so sorry about that."

Ainslie rubbed the other woman's shoulder. "It's all right. Are *you* okay?"

"Yes, I'm fine. I should go to bed."

"Aye, it probably is time for us all to turn in. We've got another big day ahead of us tomorrow."

Grace took that as her signal for them all to go to bed. She was happy to. A strange atmosphere had settled over the group since the argument, and besides, she was exhausted. She hadn't slept well the previous night, and she'd done more exercise today than she ever had.

She crawled into her tent and wriggled her way into her sleeping bag. She lay on her back, her sleeping bag pulled up to her chin. It was hideously dark. Had she ever known a darkness like this? In London, it was never truly dark. Even if she turned off all the lights in the house and drew the curtains, there was always an element of illumination that got through—a streetlamp or passing car headlights sweeping down the street. She was tempted to turn on her torch and string it up from the roof of the tent, like a normal light, but it would only waste the batteries, and it wasn't as though she could pop into a shop and buy some more. Besides, keeping the tent lit from the inside meant people would be able to see the shape of her moving inside, and that felt weird, too.

Grace sighed and rolled onto her side, her hand pillowed beneath her face. She squirmed around, trying to get comfortable. A stone or twig under the sleeping mat was poking up into her hip, but the mat was too narrow for her to avoid it completely.

How was it possible to be so physically exhausted and still not be able to sleep?

Was everyone else sleeping already?

She strained her ears, trying to tell. A couple of people were snoring softly, and she hoped that wasn't going to get any louder, either. She didn't know who it was snoring—it was hard to tell the direction—but she'd put her money on it being the older men. An owl hooted somewhere in the distance, the sound lonely, mournful.

The familiar, overly loud whine of someone unzipping their tent cut through the night, and then a rustle as the person climbed out. Who was that? Someone needing to get up for a wee—most likely one of the men. They had it far easier than the women when it came to the toilet situation.

She'd deliberately not drunk too much water before going to bed, knowing the last thing she'd want to do was crawl out of her sleeping bag in the middle of the night and stumble off into the dark, with only her torch, to find a bush to pee behind. The idea of being so exposed out here, with everyone else asleep, and nothing but endless wilderness at her back was terrifying.

Somewhere nearby, a twig cracked, as though underfoot.

She froze, her breath held, listening hard for the movement. Was the person near her tent? It was so hard to tell what direction any sound was coming from. No, she was being paranoid. Why would they come anywhere near where she was sleeping? Maybe whoever it was had needed to pass by her tent to walk some distance from their camping spot so they could take that much-needed wee?

The crack came again, and Grace sucked in a breath, every muscle in her body tense. It had been closer that time, she was sure.

What if it wasn't a person? What if it was an animal? Did they have any kind of wild animals up here that would attack a fully-grown adult? She didn't think so, but right now her imagination was running away with itself. Ainslie had wound her up about there being bears, but what about other creatures like wolves? Could a wildcat attack a human?

But then she reined her imagination back in again. She'd heard the zip go on the tent. It was just one of their group. Still, she got the sense whoever it was hadn't only got out of their tent and wandered off to do what they needed and come back again. She sensed their presence looming over her, lurking nearby, careful and cautious, not wanting to be heard.

Should she turn on her torch, let whoever it was know she was awake? She'd never felt so vulnerable.

The person cleared their throat, and then a moment later, there was another rustle, and the raspy whine of the zipper pulled back down again. Grace let out a sigh of relief. She'd completely overreacted. Sound travelled weirdly out here, and the person probably hadn't been anywhere near her, it had just felt like they had been.

She squeezed her eyes shut again and willed herself to sleep.

It was going to be a long time until morning.

Chapter Six

It felt painfully early when the birds began their morning songs and the sunlight illuminated the inside of the tent.

Grace tried to sit up and let out a groan. Her entire body ached. She didn't know how much her sore muscles had to do with sleeping on the ground, or if it was because of all the exercise she'd done the previous day, but she was in pain.

She reached out and grabbed her backpack. Preparing for this eventuality, she'd brought some paracetamol with her. She located the packet in her first aid kit and popped two of the tablets out from the silver foil backing into her palm, and then picked up the water bottle beside her. She unscrewed the cap on the bottle and put the tablets on the back of her tongue, and then took a big swig of water, swallowing them down.

Not her usual breakfast, that was for sure.

At the thought of breakfast, her stomach growled audibly. She wondered if anyone else had heard.

There were murmured voices as others woke as well, some laughter, and someone else protesting against their stiff limbs. The tent zips whined undone, and there was the rustling of the campers emerging and calls of 'morning' to one another.

Grace's bladder made itself known to her. She was going to need to find somewhere to have a wee, though the idea still embarrassed her. She was sure she'd get over it by the end of the hike. Thank God she hadn't needed a number two yet. That was going to be even more mortifying when the time came, and she'd have to bury her own mess like a dog. Once more, she found herself wondering if she'd really thought this through properly when she'd won the competition.

You're pushing yourself out of your comfort zone, her mother's voice said in her head. *That can only be a good thing.*

Yes, she needed to remember the bigger picture. She couldn't have gone on the way she had been.

She fished the roll of toilet paper and a little plastic baggy out of her backpack, sucked in her nerves, shoved her feet into her boots, and then let herself out of her tent. A few people were already gathered in the small clearing they'd deliberately left in the middle when they'd set their tents up the previous night. Craig and Isla were both up, but they were noticeably quiet. No one mentioned the argument.

Fraser was doing stretches in front of his tent. "Anyone else aching all over?"

She was relieved it wasn't just her. "Yep, me," she admitted.

"Me, too," Isla said. "My back is killing me."

Fraser rolled his eyes. "Ack, you youngsters should be fine."

"I'm not that young, Fraser," Isla declared.

He chuckled. "You're still younger than me."

It was proving to be a beautiful morning. Ainslie was already boiling up water for teas and coffees on her gas stove. "Bring your porridge and powdered milk sachets over to me, and we'll get some breakfast going."

"I'll be back in a sec." Grace motioned to a clump of bushes some way off from the gathering.

Ainslie flapped a hand and nodded to show she understood.

Grace took herself off and did what she needed, feeling horribly exposed the whole time. She used a little hand-sanitiser and a splash of water from her water bottle to wash her hands and immediately felt better. They were all in the same boat. It wasn't as though she'd done anything the others hadn't.

She made her way back over to the others.

Ainslie handed her a cup of tea. "Sugar is in the pot, if you want it."

"I'm fine without, but thanks."

Grace accepted the cup gratefully, holding it between her palms to warm them. Though the sun was bright, and it would warm up later, this morning was distinctly chilly. She was thankful for her thick walking socks and her fleece.

Scott came and took a seat beside her. He looked as tired as she felt. Ainslie, however, was full of her usual boundless energy, hopping around, making sure everyone's metal cups were filled with some kind of caffeine-infused liquid.

"Sleep well?" he asked.

"Not really," she admitted. "How about you?"

"Nah." He shook his head. "I never do on the first night, though."

She wondered if he'd been the one wandering around outside her tent last night.

He continued, "Tonight will be better, though, and by the final night, I know I'll be out for the count the moment my head hits the pillow."

"Pillow? You have an actual pillow?"

He laughed and corrected himself. "Rolled-up towel, then."

"I have one of those blow-up ones, but it was so high up, I think I'd have been better off without it."

"Just don't blow it up so much," he suggested. "You only need a little bit of air in those things."

"Oh, right." It sounded so obvious now. "Thanks for the tip."

"You're welcome."

Maybe she'd judged him too quickly. She didn't know why she'd thought he might be a bit shifty. Perhaps it was just in her nature to be wary of anyone who might be predatorial. It wasn't as though she thought she was a particularly good catch, but she couldn't help but be defensive.

Ainslie was handing out bowls of porridge made from the dried sachets they were all carrying. Everyone sat around in a circle, except for Malcolm. He took his food and sat a little way off, half-turned away from everyone else. It was strange having someone here who wasn't really a part of the group, and who showed no interest in really getting to know any of them. Was he the one who'd been creeping around last night? It wouldn't have surprised her if it had been him. She guessed he had every right not to get involved if he didn't want to.

Grace mixed some of her dried fruit in with the porridge and drank her tea. Like at the previous mealtimes, she found herself ravenous. They were burning a lot of calories each day, and she was fairly sure she wasn't eating that many. This would be a good trip for someone who wanted to lose a little weight, but she didn't really have anything to lose. She'd lost her interest in food recently, only eating because she had to. At least this might help her to regain her appetite.

When they'd all finished eating, Craig cleared his throat.

"Look, I just want to apologise for what happened yesterday. I lost my temper and made a scene, and I shouldn't have done it."

"It's not us you should be apologising to," Ainslie said, raising her eyebrows pointedly towards Isla.

He looked down at the ground. "I already said sorry to Isla. It won't happen again."

"Good." Ainslie smiled. "Then let's leave all of that behind us and enjoy our day's hike."

He nodded. "Sounds good to me."

It sounded good to Grace, too. She hated tension and conflict. She had the sort of brain that blew the tiniest little thing into something bigger—a word said in the wrong tone could become an entire argument in her head—and so witnessing something like what had happened yesterday left her feeling uncomfortable. It was normal for couples to argue, but this had been one step above just a regular couple's tiff. There had seemed to be real disdain, and dare she say it, even hatred, in Craig's body language when he'd been shouting as Isla. It wasn't as though she'd even done anything wrong. She'd only been talking to Scott.

But the air had been cleared now, and that was the main thing. It wasn't for her to dwell on another couple's relationship.

With breakfast finished and cleared away, everyone got to work packing up their belongings and taking down the tents. Those who were in pairs had bigger tents and took longer, and she was glad she'd listened to the man in the shop and had gone for one a little more expensive, that was easy to take up and put down again. By the end of the hike, she'd be a total pro at it.

Her body had loosened up over the course of the morning's activities, as well, and she definitely wasn't as stiff as she'd been first thing. In fact, she felt okay, which was surprising considering the small amount of sleep she'd managed over the last couple of days. She hoped Scott was right about the second night always being better than the first. She could do with a few hours of oblivion.

With everything packed up and backpacks back on shoulders, the group set off again. Grace was pleased this part of the walk was mostly flat, but there were some daunting hills up ahead. They weren't going to be hiking up any of the big mountains—or Munros, as they were called around here—but there were some steep ascents. They didn't appear to be following any particular path, but she'd been warned when she'd won the trip that they weren't taking any of the well-hiked routes, and Ainslie consistently had a compass in one hand and an old-fashioned paper map in the other. Grace trusted that Ainslie knew where she was going—after all, this was how she made her living.

They crossed the plateau within an hour or so and began their ascent up the hill. The steep, pathless ground made for laborious walking. Grace felt as though she was bent double under her gear, the weight of her backpack seemingly increasing with every step, and her thighs and calves burned from the exertion.

By lunchtime, the sky had clouded over.

Ainslie frowned at it. "That can't be right. There was no bad weather predicted for this week."

The sky had gone from bright blue first thing that morning, to low and grey.

"What do we do if it rains?" Grace dared to ask. It wasn't as though there was a pub nearby that they could duck into. Maybe they'd put their tents up early.

Ainslie grinned, revealing her straight white teeth. "We get wet."

"So, we just keep going?"

"Exactly. Nowhere to hide out here. It's only water. Your skin is waterproof, and I assume you brought the right clothes as well."

She had, she'd brought a set of waterproof trousers and a rain jacket, but she'd been hoping she'd get away with not having to wear them.

"Sometimes the mountains can have their own microclimate. It can be sunny only a few miles away, but thick with cloud nearby."

They reached the top of the hill and stopped for lunch, making up their own sandwiches from bagels they'd been given and adding in their own fillings from pre-made packages of tuna and cheese.

By the afternoon, the rain started. It began as a fine mist, settling on Grace's hair and skin, but quickly grew heavier, tapping on the hood of her waterproof coat like insistent fingers. The group stopped again to take out waterproof jackets and trousers, pulling hoods up over their heads to protect their hair and faces. The temperature had dropped as well, though she didn't know if that was because they were at a higher altitude now, or if it was simply because of the change in weather.

Nothing seemed to bother Ainslie. While the mood of the group grew as damp as their clothes, she kept up her high energy.

"To our right, there's a view down into the glen. Or at least there would be if we weren't surrounded in cloud."

She was only joking, but really, it was a shame they were unable to see anything. Poor Ainslie must feel some responsibility for them all having a good time. Everyone else had paid for this hike, and Ainslie must need for them to enjoy it, or they wouldn't come back, or even tell their friends. And it wasn't as though anyone could control the weather.

Grace pushed herself on, so she joined Ainslie near the front of the group.

"So, what's Jack up to while you're slogging your guts out up here?" Grace asked. "Does he just sit at home with his feet up and watch the football?"

Ainslie laughed. "You mean rugby. Nah, I'm only joking. He's still working hard. He does all the bookings, and cleans the rooms, takes care of the laundry and that kind of thing. We have daytrip walkers who come up as well, and he takes people out on those."

"Sounds like you've got a good business going."

"Aye, it's grand. We have to work our arses off in the summer months, though, 'cause it can be pretty dead in the winter. You think this bit of rain is uncomfortable, you should try walking in the snow."

"No, thanks. I'd spend the entire walk falling on my backside, I'm sure."

Ainslie gave her a curious glance. "You haven't mentioned what you do in London?"

Uh-oh. Here it was. The talk. She knew it was going to happen eventually. Her stomach swirled with nerves. She had no reason to keep things a secret—it wasn't as though she'd done anything bad—but she hated the pity and making people feel awkward around her.

"I haven't actually been doing very much," she admitted. "I've been taking care of my mum for the last few years."

"Oh no. Is she sick?"

"She was. She died a few months ago."

Ainslie's face crumpled with dismay. "Oh my God. I'm so sorry. That must have been so hard for you. Was she sick for long?"

"Yes, she was. Years. It was cancer."

"What about your dad?"

"Oh, he cut his losses years ago. He has a new family now. I don't really have much to do with him."

Her mouth dropped. "He didn't offer to help out when your mum had cancer?"

"The cancer was the reason he left—or at least a part of it. He just couldn't cope."

"I'm sorry to say this, but your dad sounds like a complete arsehole."

She couldn't help but smile. "You're not wrong."

Grace had been approaching her sixteenth birthday the first time her mother, Louise, was diagnosed with breast cancer. She remembered how shocked she'd been, how she'd thought things like this happened to other people, other families, not hers. Her mother had been strong and confident, trying hard to not let Grace worry, though of course she had. Louise had gone through a mastectomy, and chemotherapy, and after several difficult months, had been allowed to ring the bell and was declared cancer free. Grace had noticed the change in her father, however. He hadn't been able to cope with his wife's sickness, and instead of being more supportive, he'd pulled away. Even after Louise had been given the all clear, Grace noted the way he suddenly seemed more rigid around them both, awkward, as though even a kind word or hug or kiss had suddenly become a conscious effort.

Then, only eighteen months later, the second diagnosis came in. The cancer was in her other breast, and the doctors also detected some in her lymph nodes. More surgery was followed by yet more chemotherapy. The positivity that her mother had forced upon her had all but vanished, and Louise was dragged into a spiral of depression.

Despite everything, she beat it for the second time. Grace's dad at least waited until his wife had been given the all clear before he announced he was leaving her. He'd said sorry to Grace as well, and had kissed her on the head, and then walked out of their house with barely a backwards glance.

"How could you?" Grace had asked him one day, when he'd made an attempt at staying in touch with her and had taken her for coffee. "How could you do that to her?"

"I'm sorry, Gracie," he'd replied, attempting to take hold of her hand, though she hadn't let him. "I just couldn't keep going like this. This is my life, too, remember. I'm allowed to be happy."

She'd sworn at him then, right in front of all the other patrons in the coffee shop, had called him a selfish bastard and told him she never wanted to see him again.

Turned out, he'd met someone else at work—a forty-something-year-old divorcee, who already had two kids, a boy and a girl, who were almost half Grace's age. He'd slotted himself into his new, ready-made, healthy family without a second thought.

She'd been left more heartbroken than she'd ever believed possible, while trying not to add to her mother's pain.

"I don't know how you're managing all of this so calmly," she'd said to her mum one evening. "If I was you, I'd be out for his blood."

Louise had only laughed. "Maybe on some level, I'd always expected it to happen. The moment I'd got my diagnosis, I'd wondered if he'd bail. I mean, he could barely handle it when I had so much as a cold, acting as though I was only sick to annoy him, so I'm surprised he lasted as long as he did."

"He's an arsehole. A selfish arsehole."

Her mum had smiled. "Maybe, but he's still your dad, and at some point, he'll be the only parent you'll have."

"Don't say that!"

"It's true, sweetheart. We both know it."

"He stopped being my dad the minute he walked out of that door."

Louise shook her head. "That's not true, Grace. He stopped being my husband, but not your father."

Grace wished she could believe her. There was a little piece of her heart that was selfish, too, a piece that wanted to scream 'What about me?' at her dad. She was frightened about what was going to happen to her mum, and what her own future held for her. By this point, she was eighteen years old, and her friends were going to university, but she didn't dare leave when her mother didn't have anyone else. She hated herself a little for it, but her father had taken that from her as well. By checking out, he'd left his only daughter with the sole responsibility of taking care of her mother on her shoulders.

They'd had another couple of years' break before the third and final time cancer raised its ugly head in their lives. This time, they both knew it wasn't going to get any better. It was in Louise's lungs and liver now and was spreading throughout her body. The treatment became palliative, and amazingly, her mother surprised everyone. She fought it hard, and while she never got any better, she'd lived with it for several years. During all this time, Grace did her best to carry on like normal, but she was filled with a sense of her life being on hold. She couldn't go on to think about having a career or meeting someone special, because there was this massive event on the horizon. Her mother dying.

Maybe some people would have gone a bit nuts after spending most of their teenage years and early twenties cooped up inside a house with a dying parent, and would have gone a little wild with their newfound freedom, but not Grace. The very last thing she wanted was to go out partying. If anything, she cut herself off from life even more.

Her mother had been worried about what would happen to the house after she passed. She hadn't wanted any of it to go to her now ex-husband and his new family, knowing that eventually it may end up being handed down to the new wife's children rather than going to Grace, so she'd made sure they'd had an agreement in the divorce that the house was going to be in her name and then handed straight to Grace upon her death. Guilt had pushed her father's hand, and he'd agreed, and walked away with nothing more than whatever savings he had.

Grace was now the proud owner of a London house worth a pretty penny, but she was still broke. She knew the most sensible thing would be to sell the house and figure things out with the money in her bank account, but she couldn't bring herself to do it. It would be like wiping out the final memories of her mother—her mother who had been so brave and strong, and who had fought to the very end—and she couldn't do it. It felt like a betrayal, one even worse than her father turning his back on them, and so she continued to live in the strange purgatory she'd been in since she was sixteen years old.

"So, coming on this walking holiday is the first time I've really left the house since she died," she told Ainslie.

Ainslie reached down and squeezed Grace's hand. "In which case, I couldn't be happier that you were the person who won it. I hope it helps you figure out what you're going to do with your life."

"I hope so, too."

Ainslie motioned to the sprawling wilderness stretched out in front of them. Even in the rain and thick with cloud, it really was beautiful.

"I've always found I've been able to think best when I've been out here. This place is good for the soul."

Grace regarded the stunning landscape and gave a rueful smile. "Yes, I can understand why."

Chapter Seven

Surprisingly, it had felt good talking to Ainslie about things. She was sure some of the others would have overheard parts of the conversation as well and would end up asking her about it later. Maybe she should stop being so secretive. How was she ever going to make new friends and connections if she never really let people know who she was? Her mother's illness had taken up the majority of her adult life, and without that she was a nobody, a ghost of a person. It made her feel like she didn't properly exist in her own right.

As they descended the hillside, the rain finally eased off. Grace grew sweaty beneath the waterproof coat, and, as soon as the rain finally stopped, she was happy to take it off again and hook it over the top of her backpack to dry. Around her, the others did the same.

She was surprised that she'd managed to stay near the front of the pack with Ainslie. She was still aching, but not as much as she had been, and it was definitely easier going downhill than it had been coming up. Plus, now the clouds were clearing, she was able to get a view of the beautiful scenery. It really was stunning up here. It was almost hard to believe all of this was only a train ride away from London. Well, two trains, a minibus, and a good day's hiking. She wasn't looking forward to sleeping on the ground again, but with the fresh air in her lungs, and having told Ainslie the truth about her life, she felt as though she was a couple of stone lighter. Maybe it was all those feel-good endorphins Ainslie had been talking about.

A sudden cry of alarm came from behind her, and Grace spun around.

Nicola was sitting on the ground, a streak of mud at her feet where she'd skidded. Fraser was already crouching at her side, his hand on her shoulder, frowning down in concern.

Ainslie turned back to join them. "What happened? Are you all right, Nicola?"

"I slipped. The ground gave out under my foot, and I twisted over on my ankle. It really hurts."

Grace thought that was probably the most she'd heard Nicola say since they'd met.

"Do you think you can put any weight on it?" Ainslie asked.

Nicola screwed up her face. "I'm not sure. I can try."

Ainslie got on one side of Nicola, taking hold of her upper arm. On her other side, Fraser slipped his arm around his wife's torso and helped her to her feet. Nicola winced, clearly finding the whole standing thing painful.

"Sit back down," Ainslie instructed. "I've got a first-aid kit. I'll strap the ankle up for you. We might need to stop early so you can rest it for the night, and see how you are tomorrow."

"I've got some painkillers," Grace said, wanting to do something to help.

"Yes, please." Nicola smiled at her gratefully.

Grace hauled her pack off her shoulders and dumped it on the ground, while Fraser and Ainslie lowered Nicola back down. Everyone else had stopped as well, either climbing back up to see what was going on, or continuing down to join them, so they formed a circle around her. Grace pushed her hand into her backpack, locating the small first-aid kit she'd brought. She took out the paracetamol and handed them over to Nicola, who pressed out two of the tablets from the foil and swallowed them down with a gulp of water.

"Thanks." Nicola handed the packet back again.

"What's going to happen if Nicola can't walk by the morning?" Isla asked.

"I'll have to call for help," Ainslie said. "Mountain Rescue are really good at helping people out of here when they're injured."

Nicola blinked, tears in her eyes. "I'm really sorry, everyone."

Fraser patted her shoulder. "It could have happened to any of us."

Isla offered her a reassuring smile. "It's not your fault."

"Aye, the ground is muddy after all that rain." Ainslie raised her voice so everyone could hear. "We're going to have to be careful. We need to keep going, though. We can't stop here."

She was right. There was nowhere to pitch the tents, and they were going to need to stop somewhere near water so they could refill their bottles, sterilising the water with tablets first.

"Just as long as the rest of us don't have to cut our trip short," Malcolm said.

Grace was surprised not only to hear him speak, but for the first thing he'd properly said to them to be so callous.

"Don't worry, you won't," Ainslie replied.

Her voice was measured, and Grace could see how she was holding herself back.

"Thanks for the sympathy though, aye, pal," Fraser said sarcastically, not needing to hold back in the same way Ainslie had. It wasn't as though Malcolm was his customer.

Malcolm shrugged. "I paid for a full week's hike, just like everyone else."

Ainslie finished strapping up Nicola's ankle.

"I'm so sorry," Nicola apologised again. She was clearly mortified at being the centre of everyone's attention, and at having caused a fuss.

Ainslie squeezed her hand in reassurance. "It's okay. It's only an accident. They happen from time to time. Let's keep going for a wee bit and find a better place to stop for the night, then we'll reassess everything in the morning."

Malcom grumbled something under his breath and stomped on ahead.

Grace exchanged a glance with Isla, and they both rolled their eyes.

"There should be a flat area near the river where we can set up camp," Ainslie said, "and we'll have water for the next day as well."

Their progress was slower now they had to take Nicola's ankle into account. Nicola was doing well, though, and barely complained, except for the occasional hiss of air in over her teeth where she bumped it on some uneven ground. She had a set of walking poles and used them to help herself along. Both Scott and Malcolm had gone on ahead, though they were still visible as moving dots. Their position on the hillside gave them a view right into the valley, and there wasn't enough tree coverage to mean they might lose sight of the men. A winding river snaked around the foothills.

Fraser and Nicola brought up the rear, with Craig and Isla next and Ainslie and Grace alternating between leading the others and doubling back to help Fraser with Nicola.

It took another hour, but eventually they reached flatter ground near the river.

Malcolm and Scott had both already stopped. Grace saw something switch hands between the two of them, and then Scott quickly hid whatever it was away in his pack. What were they up to? Were they suddenly friends, united by the frustration of having an injured woman as part of their team? What was it about men? They never took care of each other in the same way women did. When a woman in a group of women got injured or sick, the women all rallied round and did whatever they could to help, where a man among men would probably find himself being jeered at and insulted.

She glanced over to where Fraser was helping Nicola sit down. Maybe she was being unfair. Not all men were like that. Some caring ones existed, just like there were plenty of uncaring women. It was only that her experience with her father when her mother had fallen ill the second time around had left her jaded and with a poor view of men overall. She wanted to think different, but then she saw how Malcolm and Scott had acted—not once offering if there was anything they could do to help—and thought perhaps her initial thoughts had been correct.

"This should do it," Ainslie said. "We'll set up camp here for the night and then see how Nicola is doing in the morning."

"I hope I'll be fine," Nicola said in a small voice.

Ainslie pulled a face. "Remember this is a tough hike. It's challenging for someone who is physically fit, so I'm no' sure it's going to be possible for you to do it with an injury. I wouldn't want you to push yourself and cause yourself any permanent damage."

"Yeah, and think about the rest of us, too. You'll be holding us back," Scott said.

Nicola hung her head, and Fraser glared at the younger man.

Scott needed to watch himself. As friendly as Fraser seemed, Grace was fairly sure he could throw a good punch if he needed to. That was the last thing they needed—everyone fighting among themselves. The relaxed atmosphere of that morning had all but disappeared.

Grace picked a spot for her tent, away from both Scott and Malcolm, and set about putting it up.

"Shit!"

The curse word came from the direction of Isla and Craig, and she turned to see Isla emptying the contents of her backpack out onto the ground.

"What's wrong?" Craig asked.

"Dammit." Isla gave her bag another shake. "My phone is missing."

Craig let out an exasperated sigh and shook his head. "For goodness' sake, Isla. That phone is supposed to be for both of us, remember?"

"I know, I'm sorry. It still might be here somewhere."

"Where? You've pulled everything apart." He shook his head at her, his hands on his hips, making no move to offer any assistance.

Grace frowned. "Have you dropped it?"

Isla stopped searching, let out a sigh, and raked both hands through her hair. "I'm sure I would have noticed, if I had."

"When did you last have it?"

"I'm not sure..." She trailed off as she thought. "I think I tried to take some photographs when we reached the peak, but it was too wet."

"Did you put it back in your backpack or your pocket?"

She frowned. "I'm...I'm not sure. I wasn't paying much attention."

"So, you might have not put it back in properly, or thought you'd put it in your pocket, and it dropped out?"

"Yeah, I guess so." She gave a growl of frustration and scrubbed her hands over her face. She glanced back the way they'd just come, as though considering the possibility of going back to look for it.

"We can't go back," Ainslie said, her tone apologetic. "It's too far."

"I know, I know." Isla gave a rueful smile. "Hopefully, it'll be covered on my travel insurance. It's just a pain, that's all."

Craig rolled his eyes. "Can't be trusted with anything."

Grace backed away, not wanting to get caught up in one of their arguments.

Chapter Eight

A bove my head, the moon was a curved crescent of white, the stars an explosion of endless lights.

I lifted my face to gaze at them, to remind myself of how utterly meaningless all of this was. We were here for such a tiny blink of time. Why not do what we enjoyed? What drove us? What finally made us feel like we were alive?

These people. These stupid, naïve, trusting people. It would be laughable if it wasn't so tragic.

I stared around at the tents, the bodies warm and snug inside. Exhausted from the day, they were all dead to the world. They had no idea who was watching over them, studying their every move.

It was almost too easy.

I shook my head in amusement at the illusion of security created by a thin piece of material. No locked doors or windows protecting them. The insertion of a sliver of a blade, a cut so thin they'd be lucky to even notice it when they were taking down their tents in the morning, was all it would take to reach inside. Even if they did notice the cuts, they'd never admit the truth of what it meant to themselves. They'd justify it away with the material catching on a twig or a sharp rock. Surely no one would do something like that deliberately. To what end?

People preferred to make up their own, less frightening versions of stories than admit the truth to themselves—that there was something dangerous out there. Something that wanted to hurt them. People like me didn't exist in real life, or at least not in *their* real lives, with their comfortable homes and boring jobs, and family and friends who they more often than not simply tolerated.

There was something I needed to do, and they'd made it so easy. Our society was so addicted to these things that even here, where reception was limited, they were almost never out of their hands. All it took was me noting where they put them when they did eventually tuck them away.

I couldn't allow for them to keep them. No calls for help could be made. I'd already taken care of two. One hadn't yet been noticed—the owner less obsessed than the rest, it seemed. And now I just had the others. I needed to be silent and calm, to study them sleeping just as I did when they were awake.

Their steady breathing, a light moan and a rustle as one rolled in their sleep. A rumbled snore of another. Did they dream of monsters lurking outside their tents?

I had to be careful. I couldn't risk being seen. Not now.

That would spoil all the fun.

Chapter Nine

Morning arrived. She'd slept far better, just as Scott had promised, and her head felt clearer. Though she still ached, it wasn't quite as bad as yesterday.

Grace climbed from her tent to find the group mostly awake and gathered for breakfast. Ainslie was at the camping stove, boiling up water, and Nicola was perched on a tiny fold-out camping stool, her bad leg propped out in front of her.

Grace gave her a smile of sympathy. "How's the ankle this morning?"

"Not good," Nicola admitted. "I'm so sorry. I feel like I've let everyone down."

"Don't be silly. It was only an accident. It literally could have happened to any of us."

She covered her face with her hands. "I hate there being such a fuss made for me. I mean, Mountain Rescue coming to lift me out of here. I'm sure they have far more important things to be doing."

Ainslie looked up from the camping stove and lifted both eyebrows. "You mean, like rescuing injured women who are stranded miles from civilisation and who are unable to walk."

Nicola managed a small laugh. "Yeah, I guess like that."

"I'll come with you, of course." Fraser reached out and squeezed Nicola's hand.

Nicola shook her head. "No, you stay and enjoy the rest of the hike."

"I'm not going to let a bunch of hunky rescue men whisk you away. Do you think I'm crazy? I'm not coming for your benefit."

They both laughed, and despite everything, Grace found herself smiling.

Ainslie got to her feet. "Let me put in the call and we'll see how long they'll be." Their guide went back to her tent, only to emerge a few minutes later, her brow furrowed with confusion.

"Everything all right?" Grace asked.

Ainslie put her fingers to her lips. "I can't find my phone. I had it when I went to bed last night. I'm sure I did. I remember checking the time."

Grace frowned. "It must be there then."

"But it isn't. I've completely searched my tent."

"You must have put it in your pocket automatically," she said. "Maybe it fell out when you when for a toilet break or something."

Ainslie's face was taut with worry. "That must be it, but I'm normally really careful. I wouldn't put my phone in my trouser pocket when I know I'm going to be pulling my trousers down. I've had enough experience of phones dropping into a toilet in my time."

"Let's go and look for it," Grace offered.

Scott emerged from his tent. It was the first they'd seen of him that morning. "Hey, has anyone seen a phone lying around?"

"We were just talking about that," Grace said. He must have overheard their conversation from inside the tent.

"What?" He shook his head, confused. "You were searching for my phone?"

It was Grace's turn to be puzzled. "No, for Ainslie's phone. She's lost hers."

"Well, mine's missing, too. I had it last night."

"That's strange," Isla chirped, "what with me losing mine yesterday, too."

Ainslie looked around. "Well, who else brought a mobile phone? Can I borrow it if I can't find mine? I still need to call for help for Nicola."

Grace jumped to her feet. "I'll get mine. It's still got some charge on it."

"Thanks. I'm sure mine must be around here somewhere, though. It must have just fallen out of my pocket, like you said."

Grace went into her tent. She'd put her phone next to her pillow when she'd gone to sleep that night but didn't remember checking it in the morning. Normally, at home, it was the first thing she did, but since she was trying to save the battery, and it wasn't as though they had Wi-Fi out here, she hadn't even bothered checking it for the time. The sun had been up, and she'd heard other voices, so she'd known it was morning.

She stepped in among her things, keeping her back bent so her head didn't hit the roof. Though the small tent was brilliant for taking up and putting back down again fast, and sleeping in, there wasn't much room for actually living in it. A jumper and a rolled ball of socks had fallen out of her bag, her sleeping bag half off the sleeping mat. She got to her hands and knees to scrabble among her belongings, expecting her fingers to meet with the smooth, cool glass and metal surface of her phone.

It wasn't there.

Her stomach flipped with uneasiness. She was sure she'd left it there last night. Had she seen it when she'd woken up? She didn't think so but hadn't been paying much attention. It had to be here somewhere. It was too much of a coincidence for three phones—no, she mentally corrected herself, it had been four, because Isla had lost hers during the hike yesterday—to go missing.

She pulled everything out of her bag and went through her pockets before certainty sank into her guts and solidified there.

Grace crawled back out of her tent. "Umm, this is going to sound really weird, but my phone is missing, too."

Ainslie's mouth dropped open. "What?"

"Yeah, it's definitely not there. I've searched everywhere."

"This can't be happening," Scott muttered.

"Well, it is," Grace insisted. "Somehow, we've all managed to lose our phones at the same time."

Scott folded his arms across his chest. "Or we have a thief nearby."

She frowned. "No one here is going to be silly enough to steal from each other. I mean, it's not as though we wouldn't be able to narrow down the suspects quickly enough."

"Or there's someone else nearby who's taken advantage of us when we weren't paying attention?" he suggested.

Everyone automatically peered around.

Ainslie shook her head. "We'd have seen someone else, I'm sure of it."

"Really?" Scott raised his eyebrows. "How sure?"

"Well, maybe not a hundred percent, but sure enough."

"We'd have noticed if some random person sneaked into our camp and stole the phones," Craig pointed out. "Maybe

Ainslie just dropped it while she was making a bathroom stop, like Grace said."

"But then what about my phone?" Scott asked. "And Grace's? Ours didn't leave our tents, so someone must have taken them overnight."

A shiver ran across the back of Grace's neck, shuddering its way down her spine. Could someone have been in her tent while she'd been asleep? That had been her worst nightmare about camping—the utter lack of security. It wasn't as though you could put a padlock on the zip and think that was enough protection. If someone wanted to get in, they could. She remembered Scott saying about how you always slept better on the second night of camping, and he'd been right. She'd been asleep the second her head had hit the pillow and had only opened her eyes again when the morning light had filtered through the canvas. She never slept that well at home. It normally took her fifteen different positions and a sacrifice to the gods to get to sleep, and even then, she'd wake up every hour.

For once, she wished she hadn't slept so deeply.

"This might just all be coincidence and we're overreacting," Nicola said hopefully.

"Do you think?" Scott pursed his lips. "Most of us brought phones, and now they're all missing."

"Did you not bring one," Grace asked Nicola and Fraser.

Nicola shook her head. "No, we didn't want to be contactable. That's kind of the whole point of coming all this way out here. I have my camera, and that's all we really need."

"I'm the same," Malcolm spoke up. "I don't need for people to contact me every minute of the day."

Everyone turned in surprise at hearing him talk.

"But they're good for emergencies," Ainslie said. "For situations like this."

Malcolm shrugged. "Not doing us much good right now, are they?"

Could Malcolm have taken the mobile phones? Did he have some intense hatred of them, and he'd seen people using them during the day to take photographs, and decided to play some weird trick on them all?

"Do you know where the phones are, Malcolm?" Craig asked, his tone hard.

Grace clearly hadn't been the only one whose mind had gone in this direction.

But Malcom rolled his eyes and shook his head, making a *tsk* sound with his tongue. "What would I want with your stupid phones?" He gestured to Nicola. "Besides, I want to get her out of here. I want to get on with the hike."

He had a point. He had been the one who'd acted most like he'd wanted to send Nicola on her way. How would he benefit by preventing them from doing that?

"What are we going to do if we can't phone for help?" Isla asked, looking between them. "It's not as though Nicola can hike the rest of the way."

Scott got to his feet and put up his hand in a stop sign. "Hang on. We can't give up on finding the phones just yet. We need to search harder. If someone's taken them, they might be in someone's bag or hidden in their tent. I want my fucking phone."

Murmurs of agreement rose through the group, but one person was not so happy.

"You're not going through my stuff," Malcolm said.

Scott turned to him. "If you don't let us, you're just going to make everyone think that you're the one responsible for taking them."

He lifted his chin and squared his shoulders. "You can think whatever the fuck you like. I don't give a shit."

Tensions were rising. Grace's heart beat harder, and her chest tightened, constricting her lungs. She wasn't good with confrontation—there had been too much of it in her life—and her body reacted, her face flushing.

Ainslie took control. "I think Scott is right. We should all bring our bags out here, and empty them out for everyone to see, and then we can divide up and check the tents and the surrounding areas. If the phones are hidden anywhere around here, we need to find them."

"I'm happy to do that." Grace got to her feet as well. "I'll go and get my bag and open up the tent."

Isla stood from the fallen log. "Me, too. Right, Craig?"

Craig shrugged one shoulder. "I suppose. I know I haven't taken any stupid phones, though."

She stared at her husband. "No, of course we haven't. I mean, ours was the first phone to go missing."

He gestured at the surrounding countryside. "You still might have dropped it."

"Yeah, maybe, but it's a bit of a coincidence."

Craig was right. It was more likely that Isla hadn't put their phone back in her pocket or bag properly when they were moving. Otherwise, it would mean someone had sneaked up to her bag when they'd stopped for lunch or had got into her stuff some other time while they'd been walking yesterday to take the phone. Grace was sure they'd have noticed a stranger that close to them.

"You have to do it, too, Malcolm," Isla said. "It's only fair."

He scoffed. "I don't have to do anything. Play your own stupid games. It doesn't have anything to do with me."

He went to his tent, climbing back inside, before zipping it shut after him.

Isla lowered her voice to a whisper. "What are we supposed to do? We can't force him, can we?"

"No, we can't," Ainslie said. "But, if everyone else is willing, I think we should go ahead with emptying the bags and searching the tents."

Everyone made their way back to their tents to pull out their bags and drag them to the clearing in the middle. The tents weren't going to take much searching—especially the ones that were only designed for one person—but they'd still be methodical about it.

Grace had only recently searched her tent, so she took out her bag and then made space for Scott and Ainslie to search it as well.

She did her part, going to Craig and Isla's tent to check theirs in turn. She threw them an awkward smile as they passed each other, them carrying their bags and sleeping bags out, to be emptied and shaken down. Grace searched the inside of the tent and patted down the groundsheet for any lumps underneath that might signal a mobile phone, but there was nothing. Finally, she climbed back out and searched around the outside of the tent.

"Clear," she called out to the others, suddenly feeling like a police officer or private investigator searching a scene.

"I can't find anything in either of these." Ainslie had searched Scott's tent, and then Craig and Isla's.

Scott had searched Grace's tent, and Fraser had searched Scott's and Ainslie's. Nicola had stayed sitting, resting her bad ankle.

"There's nowt in any of the tents," Fraser said.

Ainslie nodded. "Let's do the bags now."

They each went to their individual bags and emptied out the contents. Grace's cheeks heated with embarrassment at the sight of her underwear and toiletries spewed out over the ground, but this wasn't the time to worry about it.

Scott darted forward and snatched something up.

"What have you got there?" Grace frowned. This wasn't the first time she'd witnessed Scott acting as though he was hiding something.

"It's not a phone." He kept the item behind his back.

Ainslie sighed. "Come on, Scott. This was pretty much your idea. You cannae be hiding things now."

He twisted his lips and then held out the item. "It's just for emergencies, you know?"

Grace's gaze locked on the hipflask in his hand. Emergencies? Didn't this constitute an emergency?

Alcohol certainly wasn't something she'd thought to bring. Aside from anything else, she hadn't wanted the extra weight of a full wine bottle. And this was supposed to be an escape from all of that—she was running away from her demons. She'd suffered with anxiety about her health since her mother died and recently found herself using alcohol to escape her thoughts. She'd discovered herself overanalysing every twinge, turning them into something massive in her head. A headache became a brain tumour. An ache in her calf a blood clot. Blurry vision meant she was going blind. She'd had too much time to think about everything, lying awake at night, overanalysing and worrying constantly.

A glass of wine helped to silence those thoughts, but lately the one glass had turned into a bottle. It hadn't become a problem—not yet, at least—but she could already see the road she was heading down, her future mapped out. The longer she spent alone in the house, her grief and fears and worries gnawing at her edges, leaving her wired and frayed, the more she found herself reaching for the wine bottle just to get a little relief. Even though she knew it wouldn't help when she woke in the morning, her head foggy, struggling to get out of bed, and the anxiety worse than ever, she could only see short term. Getting the voice in her head to be quiet for a couple of hours was more important than how she'd feel the following day.

At least out here, there wasn't any temptation—or, at least, there hadn't been until now.

Ainslie sighed again. "It's fine, Scott. I can't stop you from bringing a drink along, if that's what you really wanted. The reason we tend to advise against alcohol is that it's more likely that there will be an accident."

"I hadn't been drinking," Nicola said defensively.

"I know that, Nicola." She sighed again, as though she was suddenly exhausted. This fierce woman with the boundless energy was finally reaching the end of her reserves. "It's just guidelines, that's all. Not hard and fast rules. You're all adults."

So, that was what Grace had seen Scott and Malcolm sharing. It was nothing sinister. But it did still show that Scott could be sneaky, if he wanted to be, and right now, Grace was starting to wonder exactly who they could trust.

Chapter Ten

While everyone else repacked their belongings, Ainslie had taken a map from her things and had spread it over one of the smooth boulders beside the river. A breeze lifted the corners, threatening to fold the map in half.

Grace made her way over. "Here, let me," she offered, holding down one side.

"Thanks." Ainslie shot her a grateful smile.

Grace jerked her chin at the map. "What are you thinking?"

"That we're going to need to find the shortest route back to civilisation."

She nodded in agreement. Things were feeling weird, and Nicola was hurt. They couldn't be expected to carry on with the hike.

Some of the others had noticed what they were doing and wandered across to peer over Ainslie's shoulder.

Their guide pointed at a spot on the map. "We can cut across here and make it to a town by tomorrow evening, or possibly the morning after."

"Okay. Whatever you think is best," Grace said.

The map meant nothing to her. It was all just a bunch of lines. She always used Google maps when she wanted to get anywhere and had never used an actual paper one in her life.

Malcolm huffed his irritation from behind them. "I want to stick to our original route."

Scott nodded in agreement. "Me, too. Why do we all have to cut our trip short just because of one person? We should divide up. Let me and Malcolm and whoever else wants to keep going continue the hike like we're supposed to, and the rest of you take the shortcut."

Ainslie shook her head. "No, we can't separate. You all signed forms meaning that you're covered by our business insurance, which also means you're going to be guided by one of our team members, so either me or Jack. You can't just go off by yourselves."

Malcolm snorted. "Why? Just because of a piece of paper."

Her tone grew firm. "And your signature. We're responsible for you on this trip. We stick together. I'm sure we can work out something where you get a second free stay with us some other time, meals and transport thrown in to make up for the inconvenience."

The promise of something for free seemed to placate him for the moment.

"Is that offer open to all of us?" Scott asked.

Ainslie sighed. "Aye, sure."

Grace felt bad for Ainslie. Nicola hurting herself and all the phones going missing wasn't her fault. She imagined the business didn't pull in big money as it was, and now they would be losing a whole week's worth of takings because of all of this. She experienced a twinge of guilt that she was on this trip for free already, even though winning it had been part of a marketing gig that had most likely brought them in new business.

"I won't expect another hike." She offered Ainslie a sympathetic smile.

"And obviously neither will we," Fraser added.

Isla jabbed Craig in the ribs, and Craig sighed then said, "And we won't either. We've done walks with you before and know none of this is your fault. You've always been great on previous trips."

Ainslie smiled at them all, but it seemed forced. "Thanks." She looked around the group. "Are we all agreed, then? We take the shortest route, and those who want to rebook their hikes can do so free of charge?"

"Sounds like a good compromise to me," Grace said, trying to support the other woman.

There were murmurs of agreement, and Ainslie folded the map up.

They all went back to their tents to finish breaking everything down and packing away. Even though it had all been searched, Grace still found herself hoping this was all some weird mistake and that her phone would drop out of her pocket.

She hated to think of the alternative—that someone among them was a thief.

THEY WALKED THE REST of the day, taking the shortest route back to civilisation. Grace kept her eyes peeled, partly for any sign of a random mobile phone showing up so they could call for help, but also for any sign that someone might be stalking them. She knew it was unlikely but couldn't shake the possibility out of her head. She remembered how she'd felt on the first night, that sensation of someone standing over the tent while she'd been lying there. At the time, she'd convinced herself she was just being paranoid. But now she started to wonder if her instincts had been right all along. Whoever had taken the phones might have been trying to figure out if everyone was asleep yet, and when they'd heard her still moving around, they'd figured they'd leave it to the following night.

There was a strange atmosphere among the group now. Everyone was that little more mistrustful. Ainslie did her best to lighten the mood, pointing out things of interest as they walked, but it was frustratingly slow with Nicola limping along, and even Fraser seemed to have lost some of his good humour. At least it hadn't started raining again. It seemed like a small thing to be grateful for, but if they'd been doing this in the rain, it not only would have increased the chance of someone else injuring themselves, but it would also have made everyone even more miserable, with nerves already fractured and tension taut.

The whole phone thing was a complete mystery. When they'd emptied their bags out and searched each of the tents, they'd proven the phones weren't in camp. If it had been one of them responsible, it meant they'd possibly even thrown the phones into the river to dispose of them.

But why would someone do that?

It didn't bear thinking about. Even harder was deciding if it was worse if it *had* been someone among them who was responsible, or if there was someone on the outside who'd been following them in order to steal from them.

Which option would she prefer?

They tracked the curve and bends of the river until they reached another wooded area.

"We're going to have to cut through here," Ainslie said. "There's no trail, but I'm hoping it's not going to get too dense."

"We'll be fine," Fraser said. "It's only a few trees."

They'd been lucky so far that day with the weather. The sun had been shining brightly, but it hadn't grown too warm either. Perfect hiking weather, Grace imagined, though she didn't have much to compare it to.

As soon as they stepped into the woods, the sunshine vanished behind the thick canopy. Luxurious, dark-green ferns sprouted from the bases of trees. Strange-looking white fingers or layered saucers of fungi clung to the sides of fallen tree trunks, together with a luxurious coating of moss. This was such a contrast to the wide-open spaces of the mountains.

Grace shivered. She preferred the mountains. It felt too claustrophobic here, and all the trees and bushes offered far too many hiding places for anyone who might be following them.

By midday, they'd already been up for hours, so they stopped in a small clearing for lunch.

"How are you getting on?" Grace asked Nicola.

Fraser put his arm around his wife. "She's doin' all right. Aren't you, love?"

Nicola forced a smile and nodded. "I'm managing. I just feel bad that everyone is having to do this because of me."

"It's not all because of you. If someone hadn't done something with our phones, we would have been able to get you air lifted out of here and carry on. Whoever messed around with our stuff is the one responsible."

"Anyway, we're still walking, aren't we?" Isla threw in. "It might be a different route, but that doesn't make it any less beautiful."

She was trying her best, but the truth was that it wasn't only the change in route that was spoiling things, it was the atmosphere as well. Both Malcolm and Scott had been breaking away from the group, striding on ahead so that Ainslie would have to shout out to them if they got too far away. Craig and Isla were behind them, and Grace was somewhere in the middle. Ainslie moved between them all, going to the back of the pack to check on Fraser and Nicola, and then picking up her pace to catch up with Malcolm and Scott.

Everyone found spots to sit, most people choosing to sit on their packs, since the ground was still damp and cold, while Nicola perched on a fallen log. They finished eating, mostly in silence, and then kept going.

The woods felt endless, and as the day proceeded, more light was lost from the sky, the shadows lengthening. It was relentless, without the changes in topography or breathtaking views. Even the river and lochs had offered a kind of mental break, a spot to stop and take a moment. Now it was growing darker, and the possibility that they'd be spending the night in between the trees was growing more real.

A crack of twigs underfoot came from Grace's left. She snapped her head towards the sound, her heart pounding. What was that? It hadn't come from the direction of any of their group. She was probably just being paranoid, but that was hardly surprising.

A flash of movement darted between the trees, and a bark of shock escaped her lips.

Those in front spun to face her.

"What's wrong?" Isla asked, her eyes wide.

Grace lifted her hand and pointed in the direction of the movement. "I saw someone—something," she corrected herself. "I'm not sure."

"It was probably just a deer," Ainslie said.

"Yes, you're probably right." But she couldn't shake that sense of uneasiness, the weight of a stranger's gaze on her back. She knew she had a habit of overthinking things, however. It was one of her biggest issues. Was she doing the same here? Had she caught a flicker of movement and her imagination had morphed it into the shape of a stranger, shadowing them, waiting for their next move?

Nicola glanced at the sky—or what they could see of it between the branches. "It's going to start getting dark soon."

"I don't want to camp here." Isla voiced everyone's thoughts. "We need more of a clearing."

"We need somewhere with water as well. I'm almost out." Craig tipped his water bottle upside down to demonstrate the lack of water inside it.

"Aye, me, too," Fraser agreed.

Ainslie spoke up. "I've taken all that into account. We're going to stop for the night on the other side of the woods, beside a river. Don't worry, it's not far now. It's just taken a little longer than I'd predicted because of our slower pace. You're going to have to trust me."

"We do," Grace told her.

Malcolm snorted, and Grace clenched her teeth to prevent herself saying something to him. She didn't want to get in an argument, but the bloke was acting like a complete dickhead.

If it wasn't for the fact that taking the phones would have gone against what he wanted, she would have been sure it had been him, and he'd done it just to piss the rest of them off.

They continued their walk, but Grace couldn't shake the sensation they were being watched. She strained her ears for any unexpected noises, but with so many others around her, it was hard to distinguish what she should and shouldn't be hearing. At least with Nicola and Fraser being the slowest, it meant that Grace wasn't right at the back. No one was going to leap out from behind the trees when they were so greatly outnumbered.

Her body was tense with every step, and she jumped at the slightest sound. Her thoughts kept returning to the missing phone, and how she was sure it had been beside her head when she'd fallen asleep. The idea of someone reaching into her tent while she was sleeping terrified her.

Up ahead, Scott drew to a halt. "Can you hear that?"

Everyone stopped with him, and Grace listened hard, trying to pick up what he was talking about over the rustling of the leaves and all the natural sounds of the woodland.

Then she heard it. Running water.

"The river." Isla hurried onward. "We've reached the river!"

Craig's shoulders sagged. "Oh, thank fuck for that."

They broke through the trees. Sure enough, they'd reached the end of the woods. There was a clearing on this side of the river, and the opposite bank led up to a hill. The crossing wasn't wide, and the water appeared shallow enough. Were they going to have to walk through it? There was no sign of a bridge.

She was exhausted and decided it didn't even matter until morning. A bit of wading wasn't going to hurt her. She had shorts in her bag, and it didn't look much deeper than that. It wouldn't matter if she got splashed.

For now, all she wanted was to eat and sleep. She wished she didn't have to go through the effort of putting up her tent, but she didn't like the idea of sleeping completely exposed.

"Do you mind if I put my tent here?" she asked, selecting a position between Ainslie's, and Craig and Isla's tent.

Ainslie shot her a tired smile. "Of course not."

Previously, she'd been happy to put a little distance between herself and the others, but now she wanted to be as close to them as possible. Hell, if Ainslie's tent was bigger, Grace would have asked if she could crawl inside it with her, but they were barely big enough for one.

Grace set about putting up her tent, joining the poles together and then hooking the interior on to them.

She spotted something and frowned, and then reached out to finger the fabric. Sure enough, her fingers went straight through it. That couldn't be right. There was a hole at least six inches high. No, not a hole. It was a slit. And it was right at the point where her head would be when she was sleeping.

"Err, guys. Can I show you something?"

Ainslie appeared beside her. "What's wrong?"

Grace moved back so their guide could get a better view of what she'd found. "What does this look like to you?"

Ainslie put her hands on her hips. "A hole."

"Yes," she agreed. "A hole, but not a rip or a tear. Check out how clean it is. Looks to me like someone has come along and cut it."

"Christ. You're right."

"Do you think it might have been whoever took the phones?"

Ainslie widened her eyes. "If it was, then the rest of us whose phones went missing would have them, too."

Grace twisted her lips. "Maybe you should check."

Ainslie turned and went to her own tent and climbed inside. "Shite," she called out. "There's one in mine, too. Anyone else got holes in their tents?"

"Yeah, I do." Scott emerged from his. "Who the fuck has done this?"

"I have some tent repair tape," Ainslie said. "It's not a problem."

"It's a problem if someone deliberately cut through our tents to steal our belongings," Scott muttered.

"We dinnae know for sure that that's what happened." Ainslie was trying to keep everyone calm.

Grace pressed her lips together, staying quiet, but she had to agree with Scott. At least it was confirmation that their phones had been stolen, and they hadn't all gone through some moment of mass craziness and lost them all simultaneously.

But the idea of someone cutting the tent while she was already inside it made her feel sick. She pictured a strange hand feeling around beside her head, while she'd slept on. Was that better than someone letting themselves fully inside her tent during the night, or not? Either way felt like an invasion.

There was nothing they could do about it now. Grace accepted the tent repair kit from Ainslie and fixed up the hole, and the others did the same. She was uneasy about going to sleep again that night, worried the same person might come along and try to steal something else, but she didn't have much choice.

They cooked up a big pot of savoury rice on the camping stove and shared it out between them. Conversation was in muted tones, and once everyone had eaten and the dishes washed in the river, they went to their tents.

Grace crawled into her sleeping bag and closed her eyes, willing the gentle rush of the river to lull her to sleep. She longed for oblivion to claim her, though images of strange men lurking in the woods threatened to follow her into her dreams.

Chapter Eleven

"**I**sla?"

The shout woke Grace with a start. She hadn't been in a deep sleep, though she realised it was morning already, so she must have been asleep for the last few hours, at least. It had taken her a long time to doze off, her ears pricked for any sounds coming from around her. Her skin crawled at the idea that someone might be stalking them, and then had sneaked into their tents to steal their phones while they were sleeping. But exhaustion must have won over eventually, and she had managed to get some rest.

"Isla!"

The shout came again, and she remembered what had woken her. What was going on? Other voices came from the surrounding tents, the familiar whine of the zips opening and the rustle of people climbing out.

"What's goin' on?"

Grace recognised Ainslie's Scottish burr.

"It's Isla," Craig said. "She's not in the tent."

Grace frowned, her stomach flipping with unease. Isla was missing? She unzipped her sleeping bag and shoved her feet into her boots, and then climbed out of the tent to join the others. Everyone was awake now and emerging from their tents, hair ruffled and faces creased with sleep.

"What's happened?" Grace asked.

Craig linked both of his hands on top of his head and looked around. "Isla's not in her tent, and I don't know where she is."

"She's probably just got up early and gone to do her business or something," Ainslie suggested.

"What? Far enough away that she can't hear us or reply?"

Ainslie frowned. "Maybe she's hurt? Was she sick? Did you hear her get out of the tent this morning?"

"No... I... I was sound asleep. I didn't hear a thing." He seemed genuinely baffled, his fingers knotted in his hair.

Ainslie turned towards the trees. "Isla? Can you hear me? Please respond, if you can."

They all fell silent, listening for any response. But other than the gurgling river, the buzz of insects, and the twittering of early birdsong, there was nothing. Grace's heart pattered too fast, and her guts twisted into a knot. She had a bad feeling about this.

"We need to spread out," Ainslie instructed. "Stay within sight of one another but keep your eyes to the ground. If she's been taken ill, and then gone into the trees to do her business, she might have passed out."

Flutters of worry danced inside Grace's chest. Isla would have to be really sick to have passed out from it. They were barely making progress because of Nicola's ankle. How slow would they be if they had to carry a sick woman along with them as well? They wouldn't be able to, she realised. Despite what Ainslie had said about the insurance and them all sticking together, they'd have to separate. Some of them could stay with Isla and Nicola, and the others could go on for help.

That was if they even found Isla.

Grace shook the thought from her head. Of course they'd find her. Where else could she have gone?

Nicola had to stay with the tents, since there was no point in her making her ankle worse, but Fraser, Scott, and even Malcolm joined Grace, Ainslie, and Craig in the search.

They separated, trying to cover as much area as possible.

Grace didn't like stepping back between the trees, the memory of seeing a figure dart between them yesterday still fresh in her mind. But she made sure she kept the others well within sight and could still hear them calling to Isla. She kept her head down as she walked, aware that Isla may have fallen and could be lying on the ground, partly obscured by a tree trunk or bushes.

With every minute that passed, a sickening certainty settled inside her. Something terrible had happened to Isla, and she was sure it had something to do with the phones going missing.

"There's no sign of her!" Ainslie's voice cut through the trees. "Everyone go back to the camp."

A combination of relief and guilt swelled up inside Grace. She was pleased to be getting out of the woods, and back in the company of the others, but she felt terrible about giving up on Isla, even if it was only for the moment.

Still, she turned around and hurried to join the others back at the campsite. Everyone was standing around, worried expressions tightening their features, arms folded across chests and lips pressed into thin lines. Most people's attention was on Craig, perhaps hoping for an explanation or bracing themselves for his reaction.

"Does your wife sleepwalk at all?" Ainslie asked Craig. "Could she have got up during the night, while she was still asleep, and wandered off?"

Craig shook his head. "No, not that I'm aware of."

Scott pointed at Craig. "How do we know you didn't do something to her? The two of you have been arguing this whole trip. We all saw you push her down the other day."

Craig's mouth dropped open. "You think I might have hurt my wife?"

Scott raised an eyebrow. "I'm guessing it wouldn't have been the first time."

"Fucking hell. I was angry, and she kept getting up in my face, and I tried to move her away, that was all. Her foot must have caught on something and she fell down. That hardly constitutes me being some kind of wife beater."

"It looked like you pushed her from where we were standing, pal," Fraser said. "Sorry, but it did. You can justify it to yourself all you like, but we all saw it."

Craig threw his hands up. "Okay, so maybe I pushed her, but I didn't want to hurt her. I just lost my temper."

"And did you lose your temper with her again last night?" Scott said.

Red crept up Craig's neck, and his eyes flashed with anger. "No, I didn't! We were fine. We went to sleep as normal, and when I woke up, she wasn't here. I didn't do anything to her, so stop fucking implying that I did, and help me find her!"

Grace stared between them. Could Craig really have hurt Isla and then done something with her in the middle of the night, when they were all sleeping? And by 'hurt' did they actually mean 'kill'? This was crazy. People didn't come out on hillwalking holidays to murder their wives, did they? Unless it wasn't planned. But then what about the phones? They'd never figured out what had happened to them, either.

"Did you take the phones as well, Craig?" Scott asked, his mind clearly on the same train of thought as hers. "Did you plan this, and so you took the phones so we wouldn't be able to call the police and get help?"

"No!" He stared around at them all as though he couldn't believe what he was hearing. "Do you have any idea how insane this all sounds?"

"Aye, we do," Fraser agreed, "but what else are we supposed to think?"

"That I'm a normal person who doesn't go around planning to murder their own wife."

"So where is she then?" Ainslie asked. "Did she just wander off on her own?"

He shook his head. "I don't know. Maybe she did."

Malcolm spoke up. "Or someone else hurt her."

They all turned towards him.

"What?" Grace said, her mind buzzing. Was Malcolm suggesting what she thought?

The older man shrugged. "Maybe she got up to take a piss in the night, and whoever took our phones is still tracking us, and he got her."

She widened her eyes. "Got her?"

He shrugged again. "Killed her."

Craig shook his head. "This is crazy."

"I thought I saw someone yesterday," Grace blurted. "Remember? I thought someone was following us."

Ainslie sighed. "No one is following us. More than one person would have seen them."

"How do you know that?" Grace threw back, her heart racing.

"Because there are eight of us, and we're hardly completely unobservant. I'm sure someone would have noticed."

"Aye, she's right," Fraser agreed. "It's far more likely Isla has wandered off and got lost."

"What about the phones?" she challenged. "Isla didn't lose them, did she?"

Craig pressed his knuckles to his mouth. "I don't know. Yesterday, I thought she *had* lost her phone."

Grace let out an exasperated sigh and turned away, shaking her head. Something had happened to Isla, she was sure of it. Why did everyone else seem to think this could be explained away?

"What about the river?" Nicola suggested. "Could she have fallen in and drowned?"

Scott shook his head. "I checked the riverbank, and there's no sign of her. There are a few footprints in the mud, but they could have been caused by any of us last night when we'd been washing up the dishes or collecting water."

Craig gave a low moan and covered his face with his hand. "Her body might have been washed away."

"Don't say that!" Grace snapped.

The thought of Isla having accidentally stumbled into the river in the dark, and having fallen and perhaps hit her head, only to be swept away in the flow, while they were all sound asleep and unaware of her struggles for survival, was too much to bear.

"Besides," Ainslie continued, "the flow of water isn't fast enough, no' by the shore anyway. If she was sleepwalking and she stumbled into the river, surely the cold water would have been enough of a shock to wake her up before she got too deep."

Craig threw both his hands into the air. "For the last time, my wife does not sleepwalk. We've been married for fifteen years. Don't you think I would have noticed by now?"

"So, what were you fighting about the other day?" Fraser challenged him.

Ainslie faced Craig, her hands on her hips. "Aye, if you want us to trust you, you need to start being more open."

Craig scowled. "It's none of your business."

"Sorry, but it is now," Scott said. "Your wife is missing, and we need the full story."

"You really want to know? Fine. We're out here trying to save our marriage, okay? Isla was having an affair for three months, and I found out. She said she'd made a mistake and she didn't want us to break up. We don't have children to keep us together, so I had to believe her. She could have left, if she wanted."

Malcom narrowed his eyes, seemingly unmoved by this story. "Could this be an elaborate plan to leave you?"

Craig snorted laughter. "What? Fake her own disappearance? Why the fuck would she do that?"

"If you're violent—" Fraser started.

He slammed his fist against his thigh. "For the last time, I'm not violent. I shoved her and I shouldn't have, but don't think for a minute that that's what this is about. We're just a normal couple who have been together for ages and who have some history. There's no crazy wife-beating agenda going on."

"I mean, it's not like you're going to say any differently." Scott looked around at the rest of them as though hoping for confirmation. "No one is going to admit to that, are they?"

Craig let out a growl of frustration, his hands locked in his hair, and he stormed off, clearly needing to put some distance between himself and his accusers.

Confusion filtered through Grace. Craig's reaction to his wife going missing seemed genuine enough, but there was always the possibility that he was a good actor. If he'd planned this all along, then naturally he'd want to make it seem as though he was upset and confused about her going missing overnight. She also thought that if he had planned on getting rid of his wife this whole time, he probably wouldn't have lost his temper with her the other day in front of them all. Unless killing Isla had been a spur-of-the-moment thing, and he'd been forced to hide the body during the night? But then that didn't explain the mystery of the vanishing mobile phones.

Could Isla have taken all the phones so no one could call for help, and then arranged her own disappearance? Was the person trailing after them—if there was such a person—actually the man she'd been having an affair with, and now they'd run off together?

It seemed like a ludicrous explanation, but at least it was an explanation. What was the alternative?

That there was a killer in their midst?

Chapter Twelve

They spent the rest of the morning searching the surrounding area, walking downstream along the riverbank, just in case Isla *had* fallen in and been washed away.

Grace's stomach lurched at every log or boulder, her mind twisting what her eyes were seeing into the shape of a woman's body, but each time she got closer, she realised it wasn't Isla. She didn't know if she should be relieved or not. Did they want to find out what had happened to her, or was it better not to know?

She preferred the idea that Isla had run off with some secret lover than that something bad had happened to her. While it was terrible for Craig, at least it meant Isla was alive and safe.

They didn't see any sign of anyone else, either. If someone was following them, he or she hadn't left any trace of themselves behind—no crushed area where they'd slept, or accidentally dropped rubbish. Grace was starting to question if she had seen someone darting through the trees yesterday, or if it was just her imagination playing tricks on her. After what had happened with her mum, she'd developed the ability to always jump to the absolute worst-case scenarios.

By late morning, the group reconvened by the tents. No one had any clues to offer.

"What are we going to do now?" asked Fraser.

"I think we need to split up," Ainslie suggested, "and send the stronger ones on for help. We have a missing person's case here, and the police need to be involved, and that needs to happen as quickly as possible. I don't know the exact statistics, but I'm sure the first twenty-four hours after someone goes missing are the most important."

Nicola lifted her hand to reply as though in class. "Hang on a minute, I know I'm part of the problem here and I'm very sorry for that, but if there *is* a chance that someone is stalking us and has hurt Isla and stolen all our phones, won't dividing up make it easier for that person to hurt someone else? Surely we're safer as a group?"

Ainslie twisted her lips and put out her hand to touch Nicola's knee. "It's no' likely someone is following us. We would have seen them. It's far more likely that Isla has wandered off for some reason and got herself lost."

"And the phones?" Nicola continued. "How do you explain them?"

"Maybe Isla was the one who took them? We really don't know. It's all just speculation, which is why we need to get the police involved as quickly as possible."

Scott got to his feet. "I can go. I can move quickly, and I'll send the police back."

Malcom stood as well. "I'll join you."

Craig was visibly shaken, but he volunteered, too. "I should go. She's my wife."

What if he had something to do with her going missing, though? He might be making his escape.

"What if Isla comes back and is hurt?" Grace blurted. "She'll need you here."

Grace caught Ainslie's eye, and the other woman gave the barest hint at a nod to show she understood what Grace was doing.

"I think Grace is right. You should stay here, Craig. It's more important that you wait for the police so you can tell them everything you know."

He stared at Ainslie. "I can do that at the police station."

"It'll be better if you're here," she insisted.

He shook his head in disbelief. "You just want me to stay here so you can keep an eye on me. You think I'm going to do a runner if I go with the others."

Ainslie kept her voice level. "No, I just think it's better this way."

Craig looked around. "So, who's staying with me? Do you think you'll be all right with a wife murderer?" He barked out laughter at his own joke.

Fraser spoke up. "Obviously, I'll stay here with Nicola. But I don't think you're a wife murderer, pal, and I really hope Isla shows back up."

"And I'll stay with you, too," Ainslie said.

Grace nodded. "And me."

"Good, that's settled then." Scott was already turning to pack up his tent. "We'll set off right away."

Malcolm snorted and then took after him.

Grace thought she'd be happy to see the pair of them leaving camp. She got up as well, intending to go back to her tent and climb into her sleeping bag for an hour. She really hoped Isla was all right. She'd liked the other woman and would never want something bad to have befallen her.

But, as she approached her tent, Ainslie pulled her to one side. "Will you go with them?" She kept her voice low so as not to be overheard.

Grace blinked in surprise. "Who, me?"

"Aye, you. I don't trust Malcolm and Scott. What if they don't send anyone back for us, or decide to complete their hike, like they wanted to?"

"Shouldn't you go with them?"

"I can't abandon an injured member of the group, and I need to stick around in case Isla makes it back, or in case we find her, and she's hurt."

"But... it would just be me and those two..."

She didn't want to admit it out loud, but the thought of being with only Scott and Malcolm made her uneasy. What if it had been one of them who'd taken the phones? Maybe not Scott, since he'd had his taken, too... But perhaps that had just been a cover? She'd seen him acting shiftily. He'd hidden the hipflask from them all. Perhaps he had other issues going on?

Ainslie regarded those left. "What if I get Fraser to go with you as well?" she suggested.

"But then you'd be left alone with Craig and Nicola." She dropped her voice a fraction. "What if Craig was the one who hurt Isla? What would stop him coming after you?"

"I'm stronger than I look. I can take on Craig." She gave Grace what was supposed to be a reassuring smile, but that did little to reassure her.

If she didn't go, it meant she would be the one left with Craig and Nicola. But maybe Fraser could stay then. She was torn. She'd seen how both Malcolm and Scott had reacted to

Ainslie when she'd talked about cutting their trip short. Would they be more likely to listen to another man?

"Besides," Ainslie continued, as though reading Grace's thoughts, "if Malcolm and Scott decide to cause problems, you and Fraser will be more than capable of continuing just the two of you to make sure we get help."

Grace let out a shaky breath and nodded. "Okay, I'll do it, but can I tell you something first?"

"Aye, of course you can."

"I'm not an experienced hiker. I lied when I won this trip. I've hardly done any hiking at all, apart from one time in Wales when I was a Girl Guide."

"Oh, okay." Ainslie gave her a small smile. "You're doing great then."

"And this is my first time camping as an adult, too. The only other time I camped was on that same trip with the Guides."

Now it was out of her mouth, it seemed like a silly thing to get worked up about. A woman was missing, and she was worrying about her hiking qualifications?

"Maybe you're just a natural," Ainslie said kindly.

Grace found herself blinking back tears, and then the two women hugged each other hard.

"It'll be fine, won't it?" Grace said, wiping her eyes. "This will be fine."

"Sure it will."

They went back to the group and told them the plan.

"You want me to go as well?" Fraser said in surprise. "I mean, I don't mind, but it seems like overkill."

Malcolm rolled his eyes. "Why am I getting the feeling you don't trust us?"

Ainslie folded her arms across her chest. "It's just safer if more of you go. What if there's another accident, and there's only the two of you? Not only will you have to deal with that, there'll be no one to go for the police."

"She has a point," Scott said.

Grace was relieved to have him on side. Malcolm was easier to deal with when he didn't have anyone else backing him up.

Malcom threw up a hand. "Fine. Whatever you want. I really couldn't give a shit."

Ainslie exhaled a long sigh. "Thank you."

There were far more important things at stake than Malcolm's ego.

Nerves twisted Grace's stomach at the idea of leaving the others behind. Mainly, she realised, it was Ainslie she'd miss. The other woman had been a fantastic support on this trip so far, and Grace could see why Ainslie did the job she did. She was good at keeping everyone calm and relaxed. But now she was going to be leaving Ainslie and would have to deal with three men on her own. Fraser would be fine, she was sure, but Scott and Malcolm weren't a great combination.

She was worried about leaving the others as well. What if something happened to them? What if there really was a killer out there, and when they got back with the police, all that would be remaining was a blood bath? No, she needed to get these paranoid thoughts out of her head. Perhaps it was best that she go on for help after all. She didn't know what sort of mental state she'd end up in if she just had to sit around waiting for the next day or two.

Grace busied herself, packing away her tent and belongings, rolling up her sleeping mat and strapping it to the top of her pack. Ainslie had divided up the food and the water purifying tablets, so there was enough to last each of them for the next couple of days. It was slim pickings but it would keep them alive, and that was all they needed for the moment.

"Are you sure you know where you're going?" Ainslie asked for the third time. She'd already handed the map over to Fraser.

"Aye," he replied. "Don't worry. We're all experienced walkers here. We'll be fine."

Grace's cheeks heated, and she stared down at her boots, wondering if Ainslie would reveal her lie, but the other woman stayed quiet. She was thankful to her for that. She could imagine how Malcolm in particular would use it against her if he knew just how inexperienced she was. It was bad enough that she was young and female. Malcolm was one of those men who had no respect for anyone who wasn't exactly like himself.

With everyone ready, Grace said her goodbyes.

"I'm really sorry you're having to do this," Nicola said. "I can't help but blame myself for all of this."

Grace gave her a reassuring smile. "It's not your fault. Try not to worry. We'll bring back help as quickly as we can."

"If only I hadn't hurt my ankle, maybe Isla wouldn't have—" Nicola's voice broke, and she ducked her head to hide her tears, her knuckles pressed to her lips.

"Don't be silly. You can't blame yourself."

Nicola nodded but kept her hand to her mouth and didn't look up.

Grace hugged Ainslie goodbye. "Stay safe."

"You, too."

Finally, she lifted a hand in a wave to Craig. She certainly wasn't going to hug him. They still didn't know for sure what part he'd played in his wife's disappearance—if any—but they had all seen him push her to the ground the other day. Whatever he said, he wasn't completely innocent.

"Ready then?" She turned to the three men, braving a smile.

Scott nodded. "Let's do this."

They chose a shallow part of the river, using exposed boulders to cross. It wasn't easy, jumping from rock to rock with the weight of her pack on her shoulders, but, other than a couple of splashes of water against her boots and shins, she managed to reach the other side without getting too wet. The woods had given way to sparser land, and they were on an uphill climb. It was past lunchtime now, which meant they only had a half a day to walk, and then would most likely have to spend another night out here, or else walk through the night. That could mean risking injury, however, though they would have to assess their option closer to the time. They needed to reach help, but not at the cost of a broken ankle. The thought of another night out here, especially without the others around her as well, filled Grace with dread.

They reached the top of the hill, and Grace turned to catch a final glimpse of the others. There were only three tents now—Ainslie's, Nicola's, and Craig's—and from this distance they looked tiny, and vulnerable, mere dots of colour on the landscape.

Grace prayed they would be okay.

Chapter Thirteen

The small group walked most of the afternoon, only breaking to tie up shoelaces that had come undone or take snacks or water out from their bags.

Grace found herself keeping an eye out for Isla, in the same way she'd done with the mobile phones, as though half expecting her to just appear and apologise for the big confusion. Not much was said between the four walkers, and she figured the men were most likely trying to work things out in their heads as well.

They'd lost time that morning searching for Isla, so while they should have reached the town by nightfall, it seemed more and more unlikely that would happen tonight. They were still very much in the middle of nowhere, but at least they were away from the trees now, and the land had opened up. Grace preferred the wide spaces of the hills and mountains. She wouldn't have admitted it to anyone, but at least this way she could check for other people. With the exception of a few craggy rock faces, there weren't many places to hide out here, and she could reassure herself that whoever might have been following them yesterday, and had possibly taken Isla, wasn't here now.

They reached the base of another hill and drew to a halt. There was a shape in the distance, silhouetted against the sky, the white dots of sheep punctuating the green landscape. It was definitely a man-made structure, and Grace allowed herself to experience a moment of hope before quashing it down again. There were no habitable buildings this far in the wilderness. No one with a phoneline they could use to call for help.

"It looks like the remains of a building of some sort. The arch at the end is still standing," Fraser said. "Maybe an old chapel or something."

Malcolm nodded in agreement. "Yeah, sounds about right."

As they grew closer, Grace could make out how the ancient stones were in the shape of a church, but there was little more to see here now than the outline. The roof and windows were long gone, the interior claimed back by the wildness of nature.

"Be careful going too near," Fraser warned them. "These things have been standing for a hundred years, but you never know when one of the walls is suddenly going to give up and topple down on you."

That was the last thing they needed right now. They had enough emergencies to deal with without adding one of their own.

Still, there was something eerie about the building, or perhaps she meant more mystical, as though they'd gone back in time and she should expect knights on horseback to come galloping over the hill.

They left the old structure behind and continued down the other side of the hill. None of this area was flat. If they weren't going downhill, they were going up, and it was guaranteed there would be another hill on the other side. Grace's initial burst of adrenaline when they'd first left the others had long faded, and now she was just exhausted.

Malcolm led the way, for the most part. Scott occasionally joined him at the front or slowed down to talk to her or Fraser for a short while. None of them were really in a chatty mood, however, and conversation seemed to be limited to either how far they'd come or how far they still had to go, with the occasional mention about how they hoped Isla had been found by the others by now.

The last few days had been hard on Grace physically, and this fast walking did nothing to help. She almost preferred the slower pace that had been dictated to them yesterday by Nicola's bad ankle, however frustrating it had been.

They walked down into a glen, and Grace huffed out a breath of resignation when she saw there was another hill on the other side. She caught a whiff of something on her inward breath and wrinkled her nose. Something had gone bad.

Scott and Malcolm were already several paces ahead, and they caught it, too.

"Ugh, what the hell is that?" Scott covered his nose with his sleeve.

Fraser pulled a face. "Smells like something died out here."

"Probably one of the many sheep," Malcolm said. "No one's watching them out here. If one breaks a leg or dies in lambing, they're just left to rot."

The stink was carried on the breeze, definitely something rotten. The moment took Grace back to the time she'd been on the way back home from a rare night out and it had been late, and she'd walked past the body of an urban fox that had been knocked down, and the council hadn't cleared it up yet. It had been the height of summer in London, and the poor fox's body had turned quickly. She'd been forced to hurry past with her shirt clamped over her face, holding her breath until she was a safe distance away.

From the direction of the wind, whatever was causing the stench was still ahead of them. They needed to go that way, so they didn't have much choice but to bear it for the moment.

Grace pulled the top of her t-shirt up over the lower half of her face to block out some of the smell.

She couldn't see any sign of a dead sheep, but there was a fair amount of foliage down here, protected from the harsher weather conditions compared to the exposed top or side of the hills. Automatically, they'd all picked up their pace, hurrying to get past the smell.

She glanced over by the bushes. She still hadn't seen anything dead, but perhaps it had died somewhere hidden among the branches. They were assuming it was a sheep, simply because there were so many of them out here, but there was plenty of other wildlife as well. It was just as likely to be a dead badger or a hare.

Grace narrowed her eyes. Something was sticking out of a clump of bushes. Was it the sheep? No, it definitely looked like a boot. Perhaps someone had a spare set of boots tied to their backpack and one fell off and landed by the bush?

Despite wanting to get past the smell, she'd automatically slowed down, trying to get a better view.

Fraser must have noticed she was hanging back. "What's wrong?"

She gave her head a slight shake. "Oh, I'm sure it's nothing. I think someone's lost a walking boot. Whoever it belongs to will be pissed off when they realise it's missing." These walking boots were expensive.

He frowned in the direction she was looking. "Maybe we should check it out."

Her stomach roiled with nerves, and, despite the warm sun, all the hairs on the back of her neck prickled. "I don't know. I think we should just leave it."

The smell and a boot... The smell and a boot.

She didn't want to think the two things were connected, but suddenly her heart beat faster and her breath came short. Every part of her screamed not to take another step towards that bush.

Malcolm and Scott had realised the other two were lagging, and they both drew to a halt.

"What's going on?" Malcolm called back to them.

Fraser shook his head. "Nothing. Just something Grace has spotted."

Scott walked back towards them. "What?"

"It's nothing." She put her head down and kept going. She wanted to grab Scott's arm and drag him with her. "Let's just go."

"Hang on a minute." Fraser took a step closer to the bushes. "There's something else here."

"I really think we should just keep going. We're going to run out of daylight." She wished she'd kept her stupid mouth shut about spotting the boot.

But Scott and Fraser were already marching over to the clump of bushes, and Malcolm, not wanting to miss out, joined them. Grace stayed where she was, her feet rooted to the ground, feeling as though ice was forming across her skin.

Scott reached the bushes and leaned in—

A cry burst from his lips, and he staggered away, losing his footing and crashing heavily onto his backside.

Malcom frowned at his reaction and, curiosity getting the better of him, craned towards the bushes as well. He clamped his hand over his mouth and twisted to face the other way.

"What?" Fraser took a couple of uncertain steps closer. "What is it?"

"A body!" Scott managed to gasp. "It's a dead body."

Fraser lifted both eyebrows. "You've got to be fucking joking with me!"

"A man. It's a man." Scott's face was pale. "A walker, like us."

Grace's mind whirred. He had to be playing a practical joke on them. Surely, they hadn't just stumbled upon the body of some poor walker.

She couldn't get her words out, unsure what she even wanted to say. "Is...was...was it an accident?"

She knew exactly why she was asking. The phones being stolen, the figure she'd thought she'd seen, Isla going missing, and now this? If the four things were connected, then it meant they were in far greater trouble than she'd ever considered. But maybe her brain was racing away with itself again. Maybe this was just an accident and not connected with what had happened to them at all.

"How the fuck am I supposed to know, Grace?" Scott threw back. "I've hardly done a fucking autopsy on him!"

Malcolm took a couple of steps towards the bushes and peered into them again. He screwed up his face in disgust and retreated.

"I'd say this wasn't an accident."

Grace stared at him. "How can you tell?"

"It looks to me like his throat has been cut."

Grace clamped her hand to her mouth. "Oh my God."

"Someone must have put him in the bush," Fraser said. "He wouldn't have got in there himself."

Malcolm frowned in his direction. "You mean someone cut his throat and then hid his body?"

"Aye, pretty much."

Scott's jaw hung wide in disbelief. "Who the hell would do such a thing?"

Fraser looked around at them all. "The same person who hid our phones and took Isla?"

She didn't want to believe it. This kind of thing didn't happen to people like them. They were just normal individuals, out walking, not hurting anyone. Wasn't murdering and dumping a body reserved for criminals, like a punishment for some kind of gangland betrayal? People didn't just slit the throats of normal, law-abiding folk, did they?

"This isn't possible." Scott shook his head.

"Why isn't it possible?" Fraser replied. "If there's a killer in the Highlands, I'd say it's more than possible."

Grace covered her face with both hands. "This is insane."

"Okay, okay." Malcolm held up both hands. "We need to calm down."

She was breathing too fast, her hands shaking. "There's a dead body, right there. How the hell are we supposed to stay calm?"

Fraser squeezed her shoulder. "Take some deep breaths."

"Should we—" She swallowed hard. "Should we check the body for ID or something? I mean, someone might be missing him."

Scott nodded, shooting a look to Malcolm. "Yes, she's right. We can take it to the police."

Malcolm appeared less than impressed at the idea. "Are you going to do it? I don't want to rifle around in some dead bloke's pockets."

"Wait," she backtracked on herself. "We should leave that for the police. There's probably evidence on the body that'll point to who killed him, and if we start messing around with it, we could contaminate the crime scene. We need to tell the police and they'll figure out who he is."

If she hadn't already thought it was important that they get to a town and find help before, she did now. Was it possible the same person who did this to this poor man was the same individual who took Isla, or was it just a coincidence and they weren't connected?

"We need to mark down exactly where we are," Fraser said. "We're gonnae need to explain it to the police and saying a bush out in the Highlands is no' gonnae be specific enough."

"You've got the map, haven't you, Fraser?" She gazed at him hopefully. She was sure he'd had it last. Losing it would be the last thing they needed.

"Aye, I do. Let's spread it out and pinpoint exactly where we are."

Instinctively, they all moved away from the body. They wanted to both escape the stench and put some distance between them and the victim. Even though she didn't know the walker, her heart broke for him. What a terrible way for a life to end. What kind of person would do this to another human being?

Fraser got on his hands and knees and stretched the map out across the ground. He frowned as he pointed at the place where they'd left the others and then traced their route. He glanced either side of him, marking the topography with what was shown on the map.

"I think we must be here." He jabbed his finger at a spot on the map. "What do the rest of you think?"

Grace had no idea. It all looked exactly the same to her. She could see that the blue lines were most likely rivers, but that was the extent of her map-reading skills.

If Fraser was right, it meant they were still farther away from the nearest town than they were from the spot where they'd left the others. They would definitely be spending one night out here before reaching civilisation. The thought of the journey ahead was overwhelming, and she wished she'd been able to stay behind with Ainslie. At least then she'd have been spared this particular horror. She prayed the rest of the group were all right. What if whoever did this to that poor man was still lurking around their camping spot. Would the group be able to defend themselves against a murderer? Nicola was already hurt, and they didn't know for sure that Craig wasn't the one responsible for Isla going missing. Ainslie was a strong, capable woman, but that didn't mean she had the kind of resources that would keep her safe from a killer.

"So, you think if we mark that spot on the map and then show it to the police, they'll be able to find the body again?" she asked.

Malcolm nodded. "I'm sure they will."

"Let's hope the killer doesn't come along behind us and move the body," Scott commented.

Grace shot him a glare. "That's not helpful."

He shrugged. "Just saying. It might happen, and then we'd all look like a bunch of idiots. You're the one who said someone was following us yesterday. How do we know he hasn't tracked us right to this spot, and the moment we've gone, he'll move the body so the police can't find it?"

"I'm sure whoever did this hasn't been following us," Fraser said, keeping his tone firm. "And they'll be long gone. No one would be stupid enough to kill someone and then hang around, waiting for the body to be discovered."

She hoped he was right.

"Is everyone okay to carry on?" Fraser asked.

"Yes, let's keep going." Grace was happy to get moving. She hadn't even seen the body properly—only the boot sticking out from under the bush—but that was enough to last her a lifetime. She could live without having to see the man's face every time she closed her eyes.

They rolled the map up and turned in the direction they'd been heading. It felt strange to just walk away from the body, as though they were abandoning him, somehow, but what else could they do? They could hardly take him with them.

Chapter Fourteen

G race kept glancing over her shoulder as she walked.
They'd put several miles between them and the body
now, but she couldn't shake the feeling of there being eyes on
her, peering down at the small group from the vantage point of
the hills, watching their progress.

She shivered.

Maybe it was only ghosts she sensed—not that that particular idea made her feel any better.

"I think we've got a bad weather front coming in." Malcolm nodded towards the mountains in the distance.

Sure enough, a grey curtain had descended over the mountains, slicing off the tops.

"Is it just rain?" Grace remembered the deluge that had ultimately ended in Nicola hurting her ankle. Those few hours of
walking, heads bent against the rain tapping on the hood of her
waterproof jacket, her feet squelching inside her boots, hadn't
been fun.

"Not sure. Looks like fog to me."

She hadn't thought it possible for her heart to sink any further, but it did. "Fog?"

"Aye," Fraser agreed. "It can be thick out here, too. Sometimes you're lucky if you can see a couple of feet ahead."

"Great." She felt like rolling her eyes. "That's just what we
need."

"There's nothing we can do about it," Malcolm said. "We'll keep going for the moment. It's important that we cover as much ground as we can before nightfall."

"How will we know where we're going?" she asked.

"I've got a compass," Fraser said. "It's just basic navigation. Whiteouts are common out here, but normally they happen during the winter with the snow. We'll be fine."

The fog crept towards them like something out of a horror film, rolling down over the mountains and swallowing up the lower ground. It didn't hit them all in one go, but first appeared as a light mist, barely noticeable if it weren't for the dampness on Grace's skin. Shortly after, she realised the view of the mountains had completely vanished, and within half an hour, even the hills had disappeared into a cloud of white.

"How long do you think this is going to last?" she called out to Malcolm and Fraser, taking them as the resident experts in Scottish Highlands weather.

"Normally only a few hours," Fraser replied, "but we're not in the thick of it yet."

She couldn't believe what she was hearing. "Seriously?"

"Aye. It'll get worse before it gets better."

Sure enough, the fog continued to get thicker. The group had spread out as they'd been walking, their stride length and pace naturally dividing them. Grace suddenly realised she was unable to see who was ahead of her. Only white surrounded her, pressing in on all sides. What if she lost the others and was stuck out here by herself? She'd never be able to find her way to the nearest town on her own. She might have supplies for a couple of days, but what would she do after that?

"I can't see anyone!" She hated the panic in her voice. "Are you all still there?"

"Aye, we're here," Fraser called back.

The fog did something strange to the acoustics. She struggled to tell which direction he'd shouted from. What if she was walking the wrong way?

"Can we slow down or stop? This is kind of scary."

She didn't want to look like a wimp, but not being able to see anyone was freaking her out. Where was everyone? Scott had been behind her, hadn't he? Unless he'd overtaken her, which might well have happened in the fog, neither of them realising they'd passed the other only a matter of a few feet away.

"It should clear soon." Malcolm's voice came from out of the white. "Just keep your eyes on the ground right ahead of you."

Grace muttered, "Good to know you're a meteorologist now."

But she didn't have much choice other than do what he'd said. She wasn't going to stop walking while everyone else continued without her. Being out here, on her own, would be terrifying, and that was without taking into account the dead body they'd left behind only an hour or so ago.

To her left, a shadowy shape darted through the fog. She sucked in a breath and reared away, but then almost immediately chided herself. She was letting her imagination get away with her again. No one else was there. It was just her eyes playing tricks on her.

She remembered what Malcolm had said about keeping her gaze on the ground directly ahead of her. Out here, it was easy enough to come across an unexpected steep drop that might take her by surprise. She didn't want to risk a twisted ankle like Nicola's.

From close behind her came a sudden thwack and a crunch, followed by a grunt, and then the heavy thud of someone falling.

Grace spun around, her heart racing. Who had been behind her?

"Scott? Are you all right?"

He didn't respond. Had he fallen and hurt himself?

She shouted to the others over her shoulder. "Fraser, Malcom! I think Scott has hurt himself."

She took a couple of cautious steps back. *This fucking fog.* She couldn't see a thing.

The toe of her boot caught on something, and she glanced down. Scott's arm! His palm was against the ground, his fingers curled in the dirt.

"Scott!" Grace fell to her knees beside him. "Scott? Scott, are you all right?"

What had happened? Had he fallen.

There was a patch of warm, wet stickiness beneath her palm, and, confused, she lifted her hand to stare down at it. The fog seemed to suck the colour out of everything, making it all monochrome, but there was no mistaking what coated her skin.

Grace screamed.

Oh my God, oh my God, oh my God.

"What is it?" Fraser's panicked voice. "What's happening?"

"Here. I'm down here." She barked out a sob. "Scott's hurt."

Hurt? Was that all? His eyes were still open, but they were unfocused. They didn't flick towards her or react to her voice.

She squeezed her eyes shut and averted her face, not wanting to admit the truth to herself.

Scott was dead.

Malcolm dropped to the ground beside her. "Jesus Christ."

Grace forced herself to look again. Malcolm put two fingers to the side of Scott's neck and held them there, concentrating. She assumed he was checking for a pulse.

Where was Fraser?

What if the same thing had happened to him?

"Fraser?" she cried. "Fraser, where are you?"

A hand on her arm. "It's okay, lass. I'm right here."

She choked a sob. "I'm sorry. I thought—" She couldn't put it into words. She was shaking violently, acid burning the back of her throat. She fought the urge to vomit. A rush of heat swept over her, drowned away by a flush of cold.

"Is he...?" She couldn't bring herself to say the words.

Malcolm nodded. "Yes, he's dead."

Fraser put his hand to his mouth. "Fucking hell."

"Look," Malcolm said, "this was on the grass beside him."

Grace focused on the thing Malcolm was holding. It was a craggy chunk of rock, the edges sharp, like it had been chipped right off the side of the mountain. One face of it—the face Malcolm held up to show her—was covered in blood.

"What happened? Did he fall and bash his head on it?"

"I don't know, but that's definitely what's killed him." He nodded down at the caved-in part of Scott's skull.

Scott's curly hair was thick and dark with more blood, and Grace tried not to think about what the flecks of white showing beneath the blood were.

Fraser shook his head. "He's lying facedown. If he's fallen and hit his head, wouldn't he be facing up, with the rock beneath him?"

"Maybe he fell and then managed to roll away?"

Fraser arched both eyebrows. "With a head injury like that? He was dead the moment the rock hit his skull."

"Oh my God." Grace went to cover her mouth with her hand and then saw it was still covered in Scott's blood. She let out a yelp of dismay and crawled away, fighting the bile surging up her throat.

She rubbed her hand on the grass, tears flooding down her face. How was this happening? Had it been another accident, and Scott had simply fallen in the fog and landed badly? Or had someone come up behind him with that rock in his hand, and hit him so hard across the back of the head that it had caved in a part of his skull? If that was the case, then whoever had done this was nearby—in fact, had been a mere few metres from where she'd been walking herself. He was most likely still out there, nearby, listening to their voices, and enjoying the fallout of what he'd done.

But why would someone do that? Had Scott done something to upset someone? He'd never been her favourite person on this trip, but he'd seemed harmless enough. No, it must have been an accident. She couldn't bring herself to entertain the possibility she'd been so close to a killer, and that someone had murdered Scott.

What about the body in the bush? Someone had definitely killed him. Malcolm had said he'd had his throat cut. That wasn't an accident.

Panic rose inside her, threatening to remove all her self-control. She wanted to escape, but had nowhere to go, and even as she crawled across the ground, air bursting from her lungs in stifled gasps, a part of her brain told her to stop. She might be getting away from Scott's body, but she was also distancing herself from Malcolm and Fraser, and she didn't want to be on her own. Being alone made her even more vulnerable.

She was trapped in a nightmare and she didn't know how to make it end. She should never have come here. She wasn't even a hiker. If only she'd never shared that stupid Facebook post, she wouldn't be in this position now.

But the others would all still be hurt or missing. You just wouldn't know about it. Her mother's voice in her head calmed her a fraction.

Grace sniffed and wiped her face with her sleeve. She missed her mum more than ever, her body aching with the loss. She'd have given anything to have her pull her into her arms and hug her and tell her everything would be all right.

If things kept going the way they were, Grace thought she might be seeing her mother sooner than she'd ever anticipated.

All those months of fear clutching her soul at every headache, or twinge of a muscle, or bout of dizziness, convincing herself that she was also going to succumb to some horrible illness, now seemed like a joke. She'd never been about to die. Right now, however, a killer was out there, stalking them.

And she might be next.

Chapter Fifteen

This one was special.

I didn't know what it was about her—the pain hidden behind a pair of pretty blue eyes, maybe—but she reminded me of the others.

The ones who got away.

I'd thought of them often over the years, sometimes with pleasure, recalling the time we'd spent together, and sometimes with regret. I'd often thought about going back, but I knew it was too risky. Always look forward—that was my motto.

This was my forward. This time now. I was having my fun, reaching my peak, but still I wanted more. I craved that intimacy of really knowing someone, understanding what made them tick. I enjoyed the change in how they perceive me, the trust morphing to horror.

I wanted to get closer, but I didn't know how.

Not everything was going to plan. There were some people's actions I couldn't control, and that frustrated me. It might cut my time short, so I'd need to work faster than anticipated.

Still, this experience had been a fulfilling one, so far, and the best was yet to come.

Chapter Sixteen

Unable to do anything to help Scott, they moved away from his body and huddled in a circle, each of them protecting the back of the person beside them.

Grace was still reeling from what had happened. She struggled to think straight, unable to hear her thoughts above the voice in her head that screamed, 'Someone murdered Scott right behind you.'

Instinctively, she wanted to rationalise what had happened, to put it into a more palatable package she could accept, but she couldn't. She hadn't stopped shaking and she kept wiping her hand on the side of her trousers, even though she'd already washed the remaining blood away with a little water from her bottle. There wasn't any more blood on her skin, but she couldn't get the memory of how hot and wet it had felt when she'd put her hand right into it.

"You okay, Grace?" Fraser put his arm around her shoulders.

She shook her head. "No, not really."

"We cannae go any farther in this fog. It's no' safe. We need to be able to watch out for each other."

Grace blinked back more tears. "How can we watch each other's backs when we can't see anything?"

"It won't last," Malcolm said. "These fogs only ever come in for a few hours. We just need to keep each other safe until it dissipates."

She stared at him. They were close enough together for her to be able to make out his solemn features. "And then what? What are we going to do about Scott's body? We can't just leave him here."

"He's a full-grown man. He probably weighs fourteen stone. We can't possibly carry him."

"We could drag him?" Fraser suggested. "We could wrap him up in one of our groundsheets and pull him the rest of the way."

Malcolm cocked his eyebrows. "Do you know how hard that's going to be, and how much it's going to slow us down? It'll take us twice as long to reach help, if not more."

Grace spoke up. "We can't leave him lying there. It's not right. What if other walkers come across the body? Think how awful that would be."

"There aren't any other hillwalkers around here," Fraser said. "We're not on any of the main trails."

"If we saw some other walkers," she didn't want to give up her tiny spark of hope, "they might have a phone on them."

"For fuck's sake, Grace," Malcolm snapped, "we haven't seen anyone else, have we? And it's not likely that we're going to either."

He was right, she knew that, but she was desperate. "So, what are we going to do then?"

Malcolm pressed his lips into a thin line and then said, "I suggest we cover up Scott's body with a groundsheet and then keep going. It's our best option. The fog is starting to clear already."

"We're still no' goin' to make it to the town until tomorrow," Fraser said. "That means another night out here. I'm worried about Nicola, too. She's hurt and defenceless, and there's a killer out here with us."

Malcolm huffed out a breath of frustration. "We don't know there's a killer. What happened to Scott might have been an accident."

"What about the body in the bushes?" Fraser threw back. "And we can pretend like Scott's death was an accident, and Isla ran away during the night, but we need to open our eyes and admit to ourselves that we might be in trouble here. Not only that, the others might be in trouble, too. What's going to happen when we spend the night out here? We're no' only going to be vulnerable ourselves, we're also going to be leaving the other group unaware of what's really goin' on."

Grace nodded. "I agree. We can't just keep going. Someone is out here, hurting people—*murdering* people. We've left the others alone. They have no way of knowing that they need to protect themselves. We could be gone days yet. What if we're picked off one by one, and none of us ever make it to get help? Ainslie and the others will just be sitting there, waiting for someone to come, and they never do, and then whoever killed that man in the bushes, or even Scott, will go after them."

Malcolm looked between them. "You both think we should turn back?"

Grace exchanged a glance with Fraser, and they both nodded.

"Aye, we do."

"Listen to me," Malcolm said. "We're supposed to be back by Saturday morning, and Jack will be waiting in the meeting place with the minibus, expecting us all to turn up. The moment we don't, he's going to know something went wrong, and send Mountain Rescue out to find us. So, even if we don't make it back, they'll still come searching for us."

It was a small glimmer of hope, but Saturday still felt like a long way away. They were due to be spending five nights out here, and so far, they'd done three. That meant they only had two more nights to get through, if they were lucky, and Mountain Rescue found them on the first day. They'd be searching a big area.

Grace thought of something. "But we've deviated off the planned route. How will they even know where to look?"

"We haven't gone that far off it," Malcolm said. "They'll figure out something happened, and we needed to take a shortcut."

He hadn't reassured her. "They won't have any idea when that happened. The hike covers almost a hundred miles. We could have taken the shortcut from any one of those miles. Think about the massive area they'd be trying to cover."

He shrugged. "Then isn't it better that we keep going so we can tell the authorities exactly where the others are so they can find them quicker?"

It wasn't only being found that concerned her, it was surviving until they were. "And what if, by the time we get back, they're all already dead?"

Malcolm sighed, his shoulders sagging. "I'll go on and send help back for you all."

Fraser frowned. "What? By yourself?"

"Yes, I'll be fine. You go back to Nicola and the others."

She remembered how Ainslie hadn't trusted Malcolm, how she'd suspected that he might just continue on the hike and leave them stranded. Surely, he wouldn't think to do that now, not that people were dead.

"You can't go by yourself," she said. "What if whoever hurt Scott and that other man, and most likely Isla as well, comes after you, too?"

"I guess I'll be taking my chances."

She shook her head in disbelief. "This is crazy. If he kills you, it's not as though you'll be able to get us help anyway."

Malcolm squared his shoulders. "He'll have to get to me first, and I have this."

He reached into his jacket pocket and produced a small knife that was part of a multi-tool Leatherman. She had one that was almost exactly the same in her own bag.

"Do you really think that's going to hold up against a killer?" Fraser said. "I mean, you saw the state of that body back there. Whoever did that was no' messing about."

A muscle in Malcolm's jaw twitched, and he tightened his fingers around the knife. "I'll be ready for him."

"Oh, for goodness' sake." Grace was close to tears. The last thing they needed was a whole heap of macho bullshit.

Panic fluttered in her chest, rising and threatening to overwhelm her. Her breath left her lungs in short little gasps, and she half bent, trying to get a hold on herself. She didn't want to lose it now. She needed for the men to take her seriously, and they wouldn't do that if she lost control and ended up as a freaked-out mess. She wished more than anything that Ainslie was here with them. Ainslie would know what to do.

"Grace, are you all right, lass?"

She jumped at the pressure of a hand on her shoulder and lifted her head to find Fraser staring at her in concern, his brow furrowed.

"Yes, sorry." She tried to keep herself grounded. "This is all a little too much, you know?"

"Aye, you're right. It is. What do *you* want to do?"

She thought for a moment. The idea of spending a night out here with only Fraser and Malcolm, and possibly with a killer hiding nearby, was terrifying. At least if they were all back together again, they could watch out for each other—safety in numbers and all that. If something happened to Fraser and it was just her and Malcolm left, she'd be petrified.

"I think we should go back and warn the others, and then figure out the rest from there. Like you said, Jack will send a search team out for us when we don't meet him on Saturday. They'll probably send helicopters. If we're all together, what can a murderer do? It's not as though he can kill all of us if we're watching each other's backs."

"He killed Isla when we were all right there," Malcolm muttered.

"That's not helpful!" she cried. "We don't even know that Isla is dead!"

"I would feel better being back with Nicola," Fraser admitted.

"So, we go back," she confirmed.

Malcolm readjusted his bag on his shoulder. "I'll keep going. I'll get to the nearest town and send help."

Grace shook her head. "No, it's too dangerous. You'll end up like Scott."

"If whoever is doing this comes after me, at least the rest of you will be safe, for the moment, anyway."

Was he really prepared to sacrifice himself for the rest of them? Or did he have another agenda?

A horrible thought occurred to her. What if Malcolm was the killer? Perhaps the only reason he wanted to get away from them was so he could follow them back, unknown to them, and then no one would be getting them any help.

No, he couldn't have killed Scott. Could he? She remembered seeing a shape moving in the fog right before Scott had died. Could it have been Malcolm sneaking up behind them?

Grace forced the thought from her head. She was being paranoid, which was hardly surprising considering everything that had happened, but it wasn't a healthy route to go down. Malcolm might just save them, and she shouldn't try to discourage him.

"Okay, fine," she relented. "Fraser and I will go back to the others, and you continue on for help."

"Agreed," Fraser said.

Malcolm nodded, his lips pressed tight. "Agreed."

The fog had all but cleared. The bigger mountains in the distance were still hidden in a thick layer of white, but she could at least make out her surroundings now.

Grace was relieved to be able to see again, but the fog lifting had also revealed poor Scott's body in its full horror.

She did her best not to look directly at it, as they set about covering the body with a groundsheet and pinning it down with some smaller stones, hiding the rock that had caved in his skull, hopefully shielding it from any weather that might destroy any evidence the police could use to figure out what had actually happened. Grace thought they'd done a pretty good job of destroying the crime scene themselves, as she remembered planting her hand in a pool of his blood and Fraser picking up the rock and showing it to them.

No hugs were given as they said goodbye to Malcolm. Grace gave him a half wave and then turned back, and Fraser shook his hand. They weren't all going to pretend they were best friends simply because something terrible had happened.

They still had a couple of hours until nightfall. They would be doing the last part in the dark, which worried Grace, but they both had torches.

Fraser was an experienced walker, and she let him guide them. She was completely drained emotionally and physically, and happy to let him take the lead. She made sure she never strayed far from his side, however, always mindful that there might be someone dangerous out here.

They walked past the spot where they'd found the other body, and Grace deliberately averted her face and held her breath. Neither of them mentioned it, but it was the elephant in the room.

"What brought you out here, Grace?" Fraser asked eventually, perhaps sick of the silence or simply wanting to distract them both. "You dinnae seem like the normal kind of hillwalker we get on these trips."

She wasn't sure what he was getting at. "Why? Because I'm young?"

He frowned and twisted his lips together. "Aye, partly, but we do get younger people walking. They're different, though. They tend to hang out in groups, and they do what Scott did and bring a drink or two with them. They're here to have fun, but I don't feel like you're here for that."

She gave a cold laugh and gestured in the direction they'd come from. "I don't think any of us have been having much fun on this trip."

His voice softened. "You know that's no what I mean, Grace."

Grace sighed, her shoulders slumped. "Yeah, I know." What was the harm in telling Fraser the truth about her past? "Will you tell me something first?"

"Aye. Whatever you want."

"Do you and Nicola have any children?"

She wasn't sure why she wanted to know. Perhaps it was simply because she wanted to figure out what kind of man she was walking with. If he was a decent father, then that might mean he was the protective kind and was better equipped to watch out for her. But if he was the type of man her own father was and had upped and left the moment things got tough, she would know not to trust him. The truth was that Nicola appeared to be younger than Fraser, and she was so pretty, Grace couldn't help but wonder if this was a second wife situation and he'd abandoned his first family, like her father had done with her.

"No, we don't. We didn't meet until later in life. It was too late for us then, and neither of us had got around to it before."

"How long ago did you meet?"

"Not long. Only a year."

That surprised her. "Really? I thought the two of you must have been together for a while."

He grinned at her. "Is it wrong to say it feels like longer?"

He'd managed to crack a smile out of her. "As someone who's never even had a proper boyfriend at the age of twenty-four, I'm certainly not going to judge someone else's relationship." She hesitated and then asked, "What about kids with someone prior to meeting Nicola? I mean, do you have any?"

He chuckled. "Not that I know of. I guess I never met the right woman until Nicola came along." He glanced sideways at her. "Now, your turn. What are you doing up here, really?"

"Trying to escape my life," she admitted.

He must have remembered what she'd said about never having had a proper boyfriend. "But not a bad relationship?"

"No, not with a boyfriend anyway."

He cocked an eyebrow. "Family member?"

She sucked in a shaky breath but kept walking while she talked. It helped, somehow, just letting her voice tumble from her lips while she focused on finding the right footing in the burgeoning light.

"My mum died from cancer a few months ago. She had been sick for a really long time. She kept getting better, but each time she fell ill again, it was worse than the last. I took care of her, right until the end." Tears pricked her eyes, and she blinked them away, not looking at Fraser, but focusing on the ground ahead of her. "Then she died, and I didn't know what to do with myself. I was left in this empty house, all by myself. I'd lost contact with all my school friends, because I was never able to do all the things they did, like go out partying, or going off to college or university. They felt sorry for me at first, but after a while, when you keep saying no to things, people just stop asking you. So, I was just a bit lost really, and then I saw a giveaway on Facebook for this hike, and somehow, I won it. And so here I am."

"And your dad? Wasn't he around?"

She snorted. "He decided not to be. He couldn't handle my mum's illness and didn't think it was fair that her having cancer was ruining his life as well. He found himself a new family and moved on."

"Moved on? You mean he left you to cope with your mum by yourself? How old were you when that happened?"

"I'd just turned eighteen. Maybe he thought that because I was basically an adult, I'd be able to cope. He'd got me to eighteen, and so his job was done."

"A parent doesn't stop being a parent just because their child is grown."

"That's what I thought, too. I'd say a daughter never stops being a daughter, but since I've barely spoken to my dad since he walked out, I suppose that isn't true either."

"I'm sorry things have no' worked out so well for you here," Fraser said.

"I'm still alive, so that's something. Better than poor Scott, and Isla. Do you think they'll have found her, I mean, when we get back to the camp?"

He shrugged. "I guess we'll find out when we get there. Let's hope so, aye?"

She nodded. "Yes, let's hope so."

They walked on in a companionable silence until they reached the church ruins on top of the hill. This time, they didn't bother to stop to take in the sight.

Grace fought to keep the image of Scott's bashed-in head out of her mind, and, though she barely realised she was doing it, she kept rubbing her hand on the leg of her trousers, wiping off blood that was no longer there.

At this time of the year, the days were long. It was a blessing in that it gave them more time to walk, and so cover more ground, but they still needed to rest. Grace's thighs trembled with every step, the strain and tension across her back and shoulders from carrying her stuff so far felt as though someone had twisted her muscles into knots, like wringing out a towel.

They stopped for a break and to have something to eat. Not wanting to waste time cooking, they settled for crackers and individually wrapped pieces of cheese, beef jerky, and some leftover trail mix. Even though she'd burned far more calories than she'd consumed, Grace struggled to eat with any kind of pleasure. She barely tasted what went in her mouth and chewed and swallowed monotonously. Her newly rediscovered appetite from the previous days had all but vanished. How could she enjoy what she was eating when people were dead?

She wasn't going to say anything to Fraser, aware that his girlfriend was back with the other group, but she was horribly worried about what they might find when they got back there. What if, when they'd left the group, whoever had hurt Scott and that other walker, had attacked Ainslie and Nicola and Craig, and then come after them?

She let out a long sigh of exhaustion, and Fraser reached down and offered her a hand. She took it gratefully and let him haul her to her feet.

"Come on," he said. "We can't have too much farther to go. Maybe an hour, tops."

She hoped that was all it was. Her reserves were down to the bare bones, and even with some food inside her, she thought her body might just give up at any moment.

"We can do this," she said, half to Fraser and half to herself.

Fraser gave her a nod and a tight smile. "Aye, of course we can."

Chapter Seventeen

They were starting to lose light.

The sky was painted like a watercolour, streaks of red and orange on the rapidly darkening blue. It made for a stunning landscape, the peaks of the surrounding mountains silhouetted against the sunset.

The dark was much like the fog had been, closing in around them, providing a place for a bad guy to hide. Grace paused long enough to rummage in her backpack to locate her torch. She flicked it on, grateful for the light, and Fraser did the same.

They couldn't have far to go now, but, in the dark, everything looked the same. It felt like days had passed since they'd left the camp late that morning. Her stomach knotted with anxiety with each step, fearful of what they might find when they got there. She wanted to hope Isla had been found, and her disappearance could be explained rationally, but deep down, she knew that wasn't going to happen.

Fraser suddenly drew to a halt and put out a hand to stop her. "Can you hear that?"

Grace froze, heart stuttering. What was happening now? She strained her ears, trying to pick up on what Fraser meant.

"Running water," Fraser continued, without waiting for her answer. "I think we might be near the river."

They were almost there. Her skin crawled with fearful anticipation. What would they find when they reached the camp? Would everyone be okay?

"Do you think Isla came back?" she asked Fraser.

She heard the shrug in his voice.

"I have no idea. Let's hope so, aye."

Grace found herself blinking back tears. "We're going to have to tell them what happened with Scott. Ainslie is going to blame herself. She'll say that she should never have let us go without her."

"Scott was a grown man. He made his own choices and he didn't need babysitting. It was a horrible accident, that's all."

"Are we going to say it was an accident? What about the other body we found?"

"We'll tell them the truth," he replied, "that we don't know exactly what happened. And as for the body... I guess we'll have to tell them. That was no accident, and people need to know what they may be facing."

"May be facing? We're talking about a murderer. These are normal people—they're not the kind who can take on someone like that."

"You think we dinnae tell them the truth?"

Grace sighed and rubbed her hand over her face. "No, we have to tell them. No good ever comes from lying to someone, even if you think you're trying to protect them. The truth always comes out eventually, and the lies normally make things worse."

She was talking from her own experience, even though it was completely different to what was happening now. It had been awhile before her mother had come clean about the cancer diagnosis, but Grace had known there was something wrong for some time before that. All the 'nothing to worry abouts' and 'everything's fine' only compounded her sense of something in the world being out of joint. She hadn't been able to figure out if it was *her* that there was something wrong with. When her mum had eventually come clean about her illness, Grace had almost been relieved. It wasn't all in her head. That relief hadn't lasted long. Once the realisation of just how serious it all was had set in, she'd wished herself back to the days when she'd thought it was all in her head.

She shone her torch ahead as they picked their way down the hillside. The rush of the river grew louder, and she wished she could see more. The moon was hidden by a thick swathe of cloud. She hoped it wasn't going to rain again, or worse, that they'd have to deal with more fog.

"Is someone there?"

The voice came disjointed and wavering across the water.

Fraser broke free from Grace's side. "Nicola?"

The voice raised in hope. "Fraser? Is that you?"

He raised his torch and shone it across the river. A white flash of an arm as it lifted to shield a face.

"Aye, it's me, Nic," he called back, "and Grace, too."

"Is everything all right? What's happened?"

"We're crossing the river now. We'll explain everything in a bit."

They stopped at the edge of the river. Grace peered doubtfully at the black rushing water. It hadn't rained since the other day, but for some reason it seemed deeper than when they'd crossed the first time. Maybe they were trying to cross at a different point. It was hard to tell in the dark.

Their torch light reflected off the surface, creating an unseen darkness below. In her imagination, the couple of feet worth of water became an unfathomable depth, that if she were to slip into it, she would be sucked down beneath the surface and never seen again.

Fraser must have felt the same way. "It's the same river we crossed earlier. The exact same spot. No reason to be nervous."

She sucked in a breath. "I know. I'm fine. It's just harder to know where to put your feet."

"Even if we slip, we'll only get a bit wet. We'll dry out again."

He was right, of course he was. But there were large boulders protruding from the surface, and she couldn't help but think of the damage that had happened to poor Scott's head when he'd hit it on the rock—if that was what had even happened. Grace had been aware of her own mortality for some time now, ever since it had finally sunk in that her mother wasn't going to recover from the cancer, and that yes, people did die and never came back. Their lives just ended. They could be a part of the world one minute, with all their hopes and dreams and loves and aspirations, and then simply gone the next. She wanted so desperately to believe there was more, and that this life wasn't the end, but merely a stepping stone like the one she was about to cross over on now, but that moment when her mum had taken her last breath and then was just suddenly no longer there, had seemed so very final.

Grace was frightened of dying. Problem was, she was frightened of living, too.

Warm, strong fingers wrapped around hers, and she glanced up into Fraser's face, grateful for the support. This was the kind of father figure she'd wished she'd had. Fraser wouldn't abandon his family for a whole new one simply because things got hard.

"Come on, we can do this," he told her.

She nodded. "Lead the way."

More figures had appeared on the other side of the bank, pale and ghostly. A murmur of joined voices as people asked what was going on. Grace did her best to ignore them and focus on the task ahead. She didn't want to slip, even if it most likely only meant getting her feet wet.

Fraser jumped to the nearest rock. They both kept their torches trained on the river, each helping to light the way. Grace pushed down her nerves, and when Fraser jumped to the next protruding boulder, she took a small leap and moved from the bank to the river. The weight of her backpack didn't help, dragging on her shoulders and threatening to unbalance her. But she kept going, taking Fraser's lead. She landed awkwardly on the next one, her feet slipping, the toe of her boot dipping into the ice-cold water, but she managed to pull it back again.

Fraser made it to the opposite bank first, and he turned just as Grace followed, helping her over the last part.

Immediately, she found herself surrounded by those they'd left behind. Fraser went straight to Nicola, sweeping her up in a bearhug, and she tried not to acknowledge the ache in her chest that made her wish she had someone who would greet her like that. Ainslie and Craig were close behind Nicola, and immediately she and Fraser were hit with a barrage of questions.

"What's happened?" Ainslie asked. "Why did you come back here?"

Nicola looked behind them, trying to get a view of the other bank. "Where are the other two?"

Before they could even answer, Craig jumped in. "Could you not get help?"

Grace's stomach twisted. They had to tell the others the truth about what had happened to Scott and what they'd found.

Ainslie must have realised Grace was overwhelmed by the interrogation. "Come and sit down. I'll make some hot tea. Are ye chilly?"

She frowned at Grace in concern and rubbed her arm, as though trying to warm her up. Grace didn't want to tell her she wasn't shivering from the cold, but from fear.

They were ushered over to the camp.

While they'd been gone, Ainslie and Craig had created a small fire, rocks from the river surrounding it in a circle to prevent it from spreading.

"I would no' normally allow a regular fire," Ainslie said, almost apologetically, "but I did no' think these were normal circumstances."

She set about boiling some water, while Grace took a seat on her pack on the ground. Within minutes, she was holding a metal cup filled with hot, sweet tea. She didn't usually take sugar, but right now she thought she probably needed it.

Someone was still missing.

"I guess there's been no sign of Isla, then?" Grace dared to ask.

She darted her gaze over to Craig to check for his reaction. After finding the walker's body and what had happened to Scott, she no longer thought Craig was the one responsible for his wife's disappearance. It didn't change the way he'd treated Isla on that first night of their walk, though. No matter what Isla had done, there was no excuse for Craig being violent towards her.

Craig shook his head, his lips stretched into a thin line, his nostrils flared. "No. When it was light, we searched as far as we could, but we didn't find anything. Not even footprints or a piece of clothing. It's like she vanished into thin air."

"She can't have just vanished. Do you still think she ran off with some man she was having an affair with?"

Craig sighed and dragged his hand through his hair. "I don't know what to believe anymore."

She'd been trying to put off the inevitable, not wanting to tell them what had happened, but they needed to know. Part of the reason they'd come back was so they could warn the others that there was someone dangerous out there, and even though the words were hard to say, they needed to be said. She was also aware of the impact the news was going to have on Craig. Right now, he could still entertain the possibility that Isla was fine, but once he'd heard that Scott had died in strange circumstances, and that they'd found the body of another man, his stance was bound to change.

"So, are you going to tell us what's happened and why you're back?" Ainslie said, looking between her and Fraser. She'd clearly picked up on the stalling Grace had been doing.

A painful lump suddenly clogged Grace's throat, and tears pricked her eyes. The others stared at her in alarm.

"Scott... Scott..." She couldn't manage any more.

Fraser took over. "Scott's dead."

A collective cry of shock rose among the small group.

"What?" Ainslie gasped. "How?"

"We're no' sure, exactly. We made it to a fairly high altitude when a fog came in. We could hardly see more than a couple of feet ahead of us. Scott fell, we think, and hit his head on a rock. It...it killed him."

Ainslie stared at him in confusion. "How could falling on a rock have killed him?"

Grace forced herself to speak. "That's not the whole story. We found something—someone—before Scott died. There was a body—"

"A body!" Craig cut her off. "What the fuck?"

"What do you mean, a body? You found someone who'd died?" Ainslie was clearly trying to hold it together, but her voice trembled. "Was it another walker?"

Fraser nodded. "Aye, but it did no' look like he died from natural causes. The body was hidden in some bushes, and his throat had been cut."

Nicola made a strange whining sound and clamped her hand to her mouth.

Craig stared at Fraser. "Someone murdered the other hill-walker. That's what you're saying, isn't it? There's a murderer out there who's hunting walkers. You said there was fog. Did you see Scott fall and hit his head?"

Fraser pressed his lips together and glanced at the ground, his fingers knotted between his knees. "No, we didnae see it happen. He was at the back of the group. We heard something, and then there was a thud. Grace was the first to find him."

"So, someone could have come up behind him and hit him with that rock?"

Fraser nodded. "Aye, it's possible. We just did no' want to jump to conclusions and frighten everyone."

Craig shot to his feet. "I think it might be time to be frightened, don't you? Whoever killed those people took Isla as well. God knows what he's done to my wife! That fucking son of a bitch! He planned all of this. He sneaked into our camp and took our phones so we couldn't call for help, and now he's picking us off, one by one."

Nicola had tears in her eyes, her face taut, thin skin stretched over her cheekbones. "Don't say that!"

He spun to face her. "Why the fuck not, Nicola? Because it's the truth, isn't it? How would you feel if it was Fraser missing? Wouldn't you think the same?"

Nicola twisted her face away, unable to deny that he was telling the truth.

"Hang on a minute," Ainslie said, clearly realising that if Scott was dead, then he obviously wasn't with the other missing member of their group. "Where's Malcolm?"

"He did no' want to come back with us, so he kept going," Fraser said. "He said he was going to get us help."

"On his own?" she asked.

Grace nodded. "Yes, he said we were making a mistake by returning here instead of carrying on, but we were worried about all of you and figured we had safety in numbers."

Craig paced back and forth, his thumb at his mouth as he tore off a piece of dried skin by his nail. "If no one saw what happened to Scott, how do we know Malcolm wasn't responsible? It wasn't as though he acted as if he actually liked any of us, is it?"

"Don't be ridiculous, Craig." Ainslie sighed and put her head in her hands. "Malcolm didn't kill Scott."

"How is it ridiculous?" His voice rose in pitch. "You all thought I'd done something to Isla, so how do we know it wasn't Malcolm? He might just have said he was going to go for help to get rid of you, when he's actually doubling back on himself and continuing to stalk us all. He could be nearby already, for all we know."

Grace felt sick. "He was walking ahead of us when Scott was killed. He couldn't have done it."

Craig stopped and jabbed a finger at her, as though she was the guilty one. "I thought you said you couldn't see anything. That the fog was too thick."

"I couldn't...but I'm pretty sure he was ahead of us."

"Pretty sure isn't sure. Maybe he made it look as though he was ahead of you so you wouldn't be suspicious of him." Craig turned to Fraser. "What about you? Did you see anything?"

"No, sorry. Like Grace says, the fog was so thick. I thought he was walking somewhere near me, but I cannae be completely certain."

Nicola spoke up, but her voice was small. "He wouldn't let us search his tent for the phones, remember?"

Craig jabbed the same finger at her. "Yes, you're right. Surely that makes him look as guilty as anything."

Ainslie shook her head. "Let's think about this for a moment. If he was guilty, he'd have done something else with the phones and then let us search his tent, I'm sure. By not letting us search the tent, he immediately made himself a suspect. Only someone who was sure about their own innocence would do that."

"Unless it was a double bluff," Craig threw back at her.

Grace's head was spinning. She didn't know what to think. Malcolm had been gruff and unfriendly, and had wanted things to go his way, but that didn't make him a killer.

"Why would Malcolm hurt any of us?" she said, half to herself. "We're all part of the same team, aren't we? Scott never did anything to him—Malcolm was most friendly with him, out of all of us—and he barely even spoke to Isla."

Craig came to a sudden halt, and then his shoulders hitched. His legs folded beneath him, bringing him to his knees in the dirt, and he bent double, covering his face with both hands.

"God, poor Isla." He burst into tears.

Ainslie got to her feet and went over to comfort him. She rubbed his shaking shoulders, but he barely seemed aware of her presence.

"It's okay, Craig. I'm sure we'll find her. She could just be lost, like we first thought. Jack will know something is wrong when we don't turn up to meet him on Saturday. He'll send Mountain Rescue out for us within a few hours. They'll find us, and they'll find her."

"She's dead!" he wailed. "I know she is. I can feel it in my heart. My poor Isla is dead."

The raw display of grief was unsettling. Tears of empathy slipped silently down Grace's face. How had this all gone so horribly wrong? Was Craig right about his suspicions about Malcolm?

"Listen," Ainslie said, when Craig's wails faded to shoulder-shaking sobs, "we're all safe here. If we stockpile and ration our food, I'm sure we'll have enough to last us another couple of days, and we have shelter," she motioned to the tents, "and warmth," she nodded at the fire. "We just have to hold out until Mountain Rescue find us. They'll be looking for us the day after next, at the latest, or, if we can trust Malcolm, they may even be with us earlier than that. We need to make sure we're never on our own, and that someone else is with us at all times, okay? Fraser, obviously you and Nicola are in one tent. I suggest me, Grace, and Craig all stay in Craig's tent, since it's the bigger one. We don't go anywhere on our own—not even to go to the toilet. It might be embarrassing having someone else watching us, but it's better than ending up dead."

"Yes," Nicola said. "You're right. None of us should be alone, even for a few seconds. That's all it took for what happened to Scott."

"If anyone sees or hears anything, shout out, okay?" Ainslie said. "Even if you think you might be imagining things. It's better that you get it wrong than someone else gets hurt."

With her words, Grace realised Ainslie was admitting their worst fears out loud—a killer was out there, and that same person might want them all dead.

Chapter Eighteen

It was a snug fit with three of them in Craig's tent.

Grace lay in her sleeping bag on the right, with Ainslie in the middle, and Craig on the far left. Not wanting to lie in the dark, after everything she'd seen that day, she'd turned on her torch and positioned it at the end of the tent. It meant anyone on the outside of the tent would be able to see them moving around inside, but she still preferred that to the total darkness.

Craig was already asleep and snoring, having exhausted himself from crying. Grace didn't think it was likely she was going to get any sleep anyway. Though her entire body ached from having covered so many miles that day, her mind refused to switch off. She was terrified about what was happening. She strained her ears, listening for any sound of footfall near the tent, but it was hard to hear much over the top of Craig's rhythmical rumbling.

Before they'd turned in for the night, they'd pooled their food supplies—what little they had left—and any other resources to make sure they had enough to make it through the next couple of days. There was no point in one of them having more than the others. Beside her, Ainslie was also awake, Grace could tell by the tense way she was lying and the anxious little breaths of air she kept making through her nose. Grace took some comfort from knowing she wasn't the only one awake.

"Do you think the other two are asleep yet?" Grace whispered. "It bothers me not being able to see them and know that they're okay."

She still had the image of Scott's dead body playing on her mind, and she worried they'd wake to find Fraser and Nicola had been murdered in their sleep and the tent would be a bloodbath.

"I'm not sure," Ainslie whispered back. "Shall I check?"

Grace held her sleeping bag up to her neck and nodded.

"Fraser? Nicola?" Ainslie spoke softly, probably not wanting to wake Craig, though he seemed dead to the world. "Are you both okay?"

"Aye, we're fine," Fraser called back. "Just a wee bit tired, that's all."

"Okay, I'll let you sleep."

They lay in silence, and then Ainslie twisted to face Grace, pillowing her cheek with her hand.

Her voice was barely above a whisper. "Do you think Malcolm might have done it?"

Grace shook her head. "Honestly, I don't know what to think. I mean, he might not be a likeable man, but that doesn't make him a killer."

"Craig was right about the phones, though. He wouldn't let us search his tent."

"Again, that doesn't make him capable of murdering someone."

She let out a sigh. "Aye, you're right. Do you think he went for help then?"

"I hope so. Only..." She hesitated, not wanting to speak her ugly thoughts out loud.

Ainslie sat up slightly. "Only what?"

"Only, if someone was following us, and killed Scott and that other man we found, wouldn't Malcolm be the next best choice as a victim? He's on his own now. We tried to get him to come back with us, but he refused."

"I don't think anyone could get Malcolm to do something he doesn't want to do."

She let out a long breath through her nose. "I know. I hope he's okay and he's already made it to a town and raised the alert."

"Me, too. We could be rescued by the morning, and this whole terrible trip will be over. I'm sorry you got dragged into it, Grace. First you lost your mum and now this... It's all so awful."

"It's not your fault. You had no way of knowing this was going to happen. None of us did." She threw Ainslie a small smile in the torchlight. "And if it makes you feel any better, I was actually having a really good time before all this started."

"Before people started being murdered, you mean."

Grace pulled her sleeping bag tighter to her chest. "Yeah, before that."

THE NEXT MORNING BROUGHT with it a clear blue sky and twittering birds. Combined with the peaceful tinkling of the river, it was hard to marry their surroundings with the possibility someone might be stalking them.

Grace had eventually sunk into a deep, mercifully dreamless sleep, so exhausted even Craig's snoring hadn't kept her awake. By the time she woke again, sunlight penetrated the tent roof, and the sleeping bags beside her were empty. Her stomach lurched, and she bolted upright, immediately thinking the worst, but then Ainslie's Scottish twang and Craig's English accent filtered through to her. She allowed herself to breathe. If something bad had happened overnight, she was sure their tone would be different.

Grace climbed out of the tent to join the others. She was relieved they were all present and accounted for that morning—all except for Isla and Malcolm, of course. There was a chance a rescue team would be with them that day. All they had to do was watch out for each other, and they would be fine.

The campfire had gone out overnight, and Craig stood over it, poking the ash with a stick to see if any embers remained so they could get it relit, or if they'd have to start from scratch. Fraser and Nicola sat outside their tent, huddled together and holding hands. They both smiled at Grace as she emerged.

"Mornin'," Fraser said. "Sleep okay?"

"Better than I thought I would," she admitted.

"Aye, me, too."

Ainslie squatted on the riverbank, collecting water for them all.

Grace called over to the other woman, "Anything I can do to help?"

Maybe Ainslie still felt as though she was working for them, but in Grace's mind they were all in this together.

Ainslie straightened, the plastic, expandable water container held between both hands. "Nah, you're all right. Just going to drop a couple of tablets into this, and then we can make some breakfast." She carried it over. "I should have done it last night, but with everything else going on…"

"That's okay." Grace gave her an encouraging smile. "I'm sure we can wait half an hour for the tablets to work."

Ainslie went to the cool bag where they'd pooled all their supplies and unzipped it, probably planning to use some of their porridge sachets and dried milk for breakfast. But though she'd opened it up, she didn't reach into the bag, instead staring down, frowning.

"Umm..." Ainslie half turned towards the others, the bag still in her hand. "Did someone move all the food?"

"What?" Grace walked over to stop beside her and joined her in peering down into the cool bag. Sure enough, it was completely empty. "Why would someone move the food?"

"I don't know, but it was all here when we went to bed last night, and now it's not."

Fraser and Nicola had both realised something was wrong and got to their feet. Fraser's arm was around Nicola's waist, offering his support for her injured ankle.

"What's the matter?" he asked.

Ainslie straightened. "The food is all missing."

Fraser frowned and put his hands on his hips. "Missing? How can it be missing?"

Slowly, she shook her head. "I have no idea, but it is."

"Maybe we just put it somewhere else," Craig said.

Ainslie's voice rose in frustration. "I didn't put it anywhere else, Craig. Why the hell would I? It was all right here. I remember going through it and making sure we had enough to last us the next couple of days. It wasn't anything exciting—just dried packets—but it would have kept us going."

Cold realisation settled in Grace's gut. "Someone took it. Whoever is doing this to us is messing with us. They sneaked into camp while we were sleeping and took our supplies, so we'd have to go hungry."

Her heart felt like a lump of ice, and her skin prickled with fear. The killer had been right here, moving around their tents while they'd been sleeping inside.

"Why didn't anyone hear anything?" Fraser asked.

Ainslie glanced to Craig. "We couldn't have heard a thing over Craig's snoring."

Craig's mouth dropped open. "Don't blame me! I can't help it if I snore. I was exhausted."

"We all were," Nicola said, "which is probably why none of us heard anything."

Ainslie took a breath. "It's okay. We can manage a day or two without food. It won't be fun, but it shouldn't be much longer than that. Help will be with us soon."

Grace was already hungry. All the calories she'd burned the previous day hadn't been replaced, and her hunger already felt like a gaping hole in her gut, insistent stomach acid burning the back of her throat. But it wasn't so much the thought of going without food that was bothering her, it was more the thought that the killer had been right there, looking down on them while they slept, defenceless.

It meant they weren't here alone.

"It's not just about the food, though, is it?" she said. "If someone came into camp and took it, it's most likely going to be whoever has been stalking us, the same person who took our phones, and who might have taken Isla and killed Scott, and possibly even murdered that other walker we found."

Ainslie rubbed her hand across her lips as she thought. "If he's here, at least it might have meant he left Malcolm alone, and so Malcolm might have got help by now."

"Not necessarily." She didn't want to be the bearer of bad news, but they all needed to be realistic about what they were up against. "He could easily have killed Malcolm and then turned around and followed me and Fraser back here."

Grace took in the sight of the rounded eyes and pale faces. Nicola glanced over her shoulder, as though she thought she might suddenly find the killer right behind her.

"If we don't get out of here today," Ainslie said, "we should have two of us keeping watch tonight."

Grace nodded. "Good idea."

Craig stared between them. "So, we're just going to stay here, then? Even though whoever is doing this knows exactly where we are?"

"What will we achieve by trying to move?" Grace said. "This person, whoever the hell they are, will only come after us."

She couldn't tell if she would feel more or less vulnerable by staying in one place.

"Plus," Fraser added, "we've still got Nicola's injury to think about. She can't hike that kind of distance, not with a sprained ankle."

"I agree," Ainslie said. "Also, if we move and there is a chance Malcolm *has* got help, then we'll only be making it harder for the rescue team to find us."

Craig folded his arms across his chest, his lower lip jutting in a pout, making him look like a sulky schoolboy, even though he must be in his late thirties. "That's if it wasn't Malcolm who took our food in the first place."

Grace shook her head. "Why would Malcolm do that?"

Craig threw both hands in the air. "Because he's a nutter. He likes messing with us!"

"I really don't think it was Malcolm." She just couldn't picture it. He was too no-nonsense to be playing stupid tricks like that. It didn't mean she was correct, but the idea of it being Malcolm didn't sit right with her.

"Aye," Ainslie agreed. "It's far more likely to be someone we don't know. You said you found a body that had already been there a few days, right? So, it makes more sense that it's someone up here who's got a thing against hillwalkers. He must have spotted our group and fixated on us, for some reason."

Grace's stomach rumbled again, and even though she'd managed a couple of hours sleep, her head was still foggy with tiredness. She wished she could climb into her bed at home, lock all the windows and doors, and not emerge for a week.

"Is nothing left? No tea bags or coffee?" Grace peered hopefully into the bag, as though hoping something would just materialise.

Ainslie shook her head, pursing her lips. "No, sorry."

"I still have a couple of cereal bars," Craig admitted. "I kept them in my bag. Sorry."

They'd all pooled everything last night, but Craig had clearly held some back. Right at that moment, though, she could hardly be angry. His selfishness meant they were at least going to be able to put something in their stomachs, even if it was only a couple of mouthfuls.

"Anything would be appreciated right now," she said.

Craig nodded and got up to head back into the tent to rifle through his stuff.

Ainslie let out a long sigh but then pasted on a smile. "Water and a mouthful of cereal bar it is then." She was trying to sound jovial, but the lack of food was depressing. Then her expression crumpled, and she reached for the empty cool bag.

Grace's heart sank. "What now?"

She unzipped the smaller pocket on the front of the bag. "I just remembered the water purification tablets were in here, too." She peered inside, then delved in with her hand, and finally tipped the bag upside down and shook it, as though hoping they might magically appear, falling through the air.

Grace steepled her fingers and pressed them to her lips. "He took the sterilising tablets as well." It wasn't a question.

"For the water?" Fraser asked.

"Aye. That's more problematic than the food."

"The water here must be pretty clean, though, isn't it?" Grace glanced over at the rushing, burbling river. The water was crystal clear, offering them a view right down to the stony riverbed.

Ainslie shrugged, her whole body slumped over, as though she was finally defeated. "You never know. If a sheep or something has died upstream, it could easily be contaminating the water without us being able to see anything."

Though it was still early, the day was already warm. Grace gazed up at the sky doubtfully. It certainly didn't look as though it was going to rain anytime soon, and if the sun got much hotter, they were going to get thirsty. If they did decide to try to hike out of here, they wouldn't get far with nothing to drink.

"We're going to need water," Grace said.

Fraser got to his feet. "It's okay. It's no' a total disaster. We're just goin' to have to boil the water before we can drink it. We can manage."

Ainslie gave a sigh. "Let's hope the gas cannisters hold out long enough."

Grace could suddenly see her future if they weren't found. No supplies, with no way to boil water so they were forced to drink it dirty, terrified, starving, exhausted, and sick. Was this the son of a bitch's plan? Did he want to push them to their absolute extreme prior to killing them off?

No, she forced herself away from that train of thought. Help would come before that happened. Wouldn't it? Even if Malcolm never made it to the town to raise the alarm, as soon as they didn't turn up to meet Jack on Saturday—which she realised was tomorrow—Jack would know something had happened. How hard would it be to find them out here? Of course, they weren't on the route they'd planned, and without Malcolm to tell them exactly where they'd camped, it would make finding them far harder.

She didn't want to think too hard about it. If Malcolm didn't make it back, it would most likely mean one of two things—whoever was doing this to them had got Malcolm like he had Scott, and so Malcolm was dead as well, or else it meant that Malcolm was the one responsible for this happening to them.

Was it better to think of it being Malcolm out there, sneaking into their camp, than it was some faceless stranger?

Ainslie lit the camp stove to boil the water she'd collected. They would need to let it cool again before they could even drink it. Craig shared out the cereal bars he'd stashed away, but they literally lasted a couple of mouthfuls and were gone in seconds.

It was hard sitting around, waiting, without even so much as a cup of tea to break up the time.

"I could go and collect some more firewood," Craig offered. "Someone could come with me."

"You might lose sight of each other between the trees, or one of you get distracted by something." Fresh panic tightened Grace's chest. "It would only take them a second." She remembered how quickly it had happened with Scott, how one moment, they'd been walking, and the next he was dead. The same thing could happen here, and she couldn't stand the thought of it.

"The gas on the stove isn't going to last forever," he pointed out. "And if we need it for our drinking water now, it's important we have a backup."

"There will be some twigs and sticks nearby," Ainslie said. "You don't need to go right back into the woods."

"Aye." Fraser rose to his feet. "I'll give ye a hand."

Ainslie nodded. "Okay, but make sure we can see you at all times."

Collecting the firewood had less to do with needing the fire, and everything to do with people needing to feel like they were doing something practical. It was bad for the soul to feel as though you were completely helpless. Grace remembered how it had been when her mother had been really sick. If Grace had just sat around, she'd worry herself into depression, but at least if she could feel as though she was doing something productive, it would keep both her mind and body occupied.

There was something to be said about not having so much time to dwell. After the funeral, her dad had tried to step in, wanting to help make arrangements, but she hadn't let him. That was her job, not his. He'd resigned the day he'd chosen another family over the one he'd helped to create, and she wasn't going to let him do anything to ease his guilty conscience or take away any of the things she needed to distract herself.

How would her dad feel if she died up here, she couldn't help but wonder? Would he feel bad about it? Would he miss her? Or would she just be another loose end that had tied itself up so he could go on with his far less messy life?

A knot in the middle of her chest tightened at the thought of her father. If she survived this, could she ever bring herself to forgive him for what he did to her mother? She didn't think so, though she also recognised that squeezing around her heart as something akin to regret.

Chapter Nineteen

When the boiled water had cooled enough for it to be drinkable, Ainslie filled up each of their water bottles, including her own, with the clean water.

The men returned with armfuls of sticks, and they got the campfire burning again. Even though the day was warm, there was something comforting about the way the flames licked into the sky. It made their little spot more homely and gave them something to focus on.

They took turns tending the fire or watching out from the riverbank for any sign of either a rescue team or even other walkers. All they needed was for another hillwalker with a mobile phone to have taken the route, and then they'd be able to call for help. But as the hours passed by, there was no sign of anyone—not even the person who'd stolen their supplies during the night.

Grace sat a short distance from the camp, staring across the river up at the hill that she and Fraser had climbed down the previous evening. More accurately, she stared at the sky above the peak of the hill, praying she would hear the drone of a helicopter or that it would appear as a dark blob against the blue of the sky.

She made sure neither she, nor any of the others, went out of sight for even a few seconds. They needed to watch out for each other more than ever right now. It was horrible to think whoever had done that to Scott might be watching them from some unseen position, figuring out who he'd take down next. Did he have a plan and was picking them off in a preordained order? Or was he purely opportunistic and simply went for whoever had made themselves most vulnerable?

Like Scott walking at the back of the group...

If she'd been walking any slower, would it have been her head that had been bashed in with a rock? She shuddered at the thought.

Someone moving farther downstream caught her eye, and Grace sat up, craning her neck. The figure straightened and turned to walk towards the camp.

Grace frowned. It was Nicola carrying the container for the water, but something was different about her. For a moment, Grace couldn't pin down what it was, but then it dawned on her. Nicola's limp had vanished. She appeared to be walking just fine.

"Hey," Grace called over to her. "You shouldn't go to the river on your own. You can't keep an eye out when you're bending down."

"Oh, it's fine," Nicola said dismissively. "Everyone can see me from over there, I'm sure."

Grace looked back over her shoulder to where everyone else was sitting around the campfire. They couldn't see her from that vantage point, not fully—the tents and a couple of trees blocked the way. Anything might have happened. But then Nicola hadn't had the shock of seeing Scott, or the body they'd found in the bushes, so even though she knew Isla was missing, maybe she just wasn't taking this whole thing as seriously?

"Is your ankle better then?" She nodded down at Nicola's injured leg.

It had been a couple of days since Nicola had hurt it now. Grace's heart sparked with hope. If Nicola was better, they could all walk out of here together. She felt bad that they'd be leaving Isla when they still didn't know what had happened to her, but at least then they could all go for help.

Nicola wrinkled her nose. "No, not really. I still can't put any weight on it."

Her comment surprised Grace. "Really? I thought I saw you walking on it."

The other woman's gaze shifted away from hers, and her shoulders lifted in a shrug. "Oh, I was putting all my weight on the other foot."

"Right, of course."

Did she believe her? What possible reason would Nicola have to lie? But the bottle of water she was carrying was heavy, and she was having to hold it between both hands. She'd definitely been walking straight a moment ago, but now Nicola was lurching with the water container held on her good side. Maybe Grace had been mistaken. She wasn't sure she could even trust her own eyes at the moment. She'd been through a lot—they all had—and were stressed and frightened and tired. It was hardly surprising that she was mistaken when she'd thought she'd seen Nicola walking perfectly well.

"Sorry." Grace rubbed her eyes. "I feel a bit like I'm losing my mind."

"That's okay. I think we're all feeling a little bit like that."

"Let me take that for you," Grace offered, reaching for the water container. Though it weighed hardly anything empty, it was heavy when it was full.

Nicola smiled gratefully and handed it over. "Thanks."

"Get one of us to do it next time," she said. "If you're still in pain, you should be resting."

"Yeah, I know." She let out a sigh. "I only wanted to do something to contribute. I feel horrible that we're all here because of me."

"We're not. This isn't your fault."

The corners of Nicola's mouth turned down. "I wish I could believe that, but thanks."

There had been lots of things that had brought them to this moment. Nicola's ankle was simply a contributing factor.

They joined the others back at the camp and set about boiling more water. It was better to have too much than too little.

It wasn't easy, waiting for the hours to pass, keeping an eye on the sky for any signs of a helicopter that might mean people were looking for them. With each passing hour, Grace's hunger increased, and she even considered if it was possible to catch a fish in the river. It was only shallow, but surely even shallow parts had fish in them. Not that they had a fishing line, or hook, or a net, even.

Craig paced the camp, while Nicola and Fraser climbed back inside their tent, perhaps planning on catching up on some sleep, or maybe even just having some alone time.

She remembered what Fraser had told her about how him and Nicola had only recently met. Was it because they were older that she'd assumed they'd been together far longer? She couldn't imagine how Craig was feeling with Isla still missing.

Even if it was true about Isla having had an affair, they'd obviously made the decision that their marriage was worth fighting for. How tragic for it to end like this.

She caught sight of Ainslie, sitting with her arms wrapped around her stomach. Her expression was tight, her features pinched.

"Hungry?" Grace asked, trying to sound sympathetic, despite being starving herself.

"Aye, but I've also got stomach ache." Ainslie rubbed her non-existent belly and then picked up her water bottle and took a sip. "Maybe it's just from not eating."

Ainslie did look pale.

Grace frowned and got to her feet. She crossed over to where Ainslie was sitting and placed her palm against Ainslie's forehead. Ainslie's skin felt cool, but she was sweating.

"Hmm, you don't have a temperature, but you're definitely feeling clammy. Maybe you should go and lie down in the tent for a little while, try to get some more sleep. I'll keep an eye on everything out here, and Craig is here, too."

"Aye, I think I might do that. Call out if ye need me, though," she added.

"We'll be fine." Grace risked a smile. "Get some rest."

She could have done with a lie down herself, but she was used to working through exhaustion. In those final months of her mother's life, right before she'd gone into a hospice on palliative care, there wasn't a single night that passed when she wasn't up, looked after her mother because her mum was in too much pain to sleep, or she'd had an accident in the bed, or some other thing that needed taking care of. It hadn't been easy, but she'd pushed through it because she'd had no other choice, just like what was happening now.

Grace discovered herself alone with Craig. He was still wandering around, clearly having itchy feet after being stuck in the same place for too long. He stood with his back to her, looking out over the river.

She hoped she wouldn't have to worry about him. She still hadn't fully wiped clean any suspicions she might have had about him hurting Isla. Yes, he'd put on a good show, and he was here with the others when Scott was killed, but there was still the possibility that Isla going missing had nothing to do with anything else that had happened.

If that was the case, she was sitting here, alone, with a man who might have murdered his wife.

She glanced towards one of the tents. It was okay. Fraser and Nicola were right there. Not that she really expected Craig to do anything to hurt her, but if he did try something, they were only separated from the others by a thin piece of material, and they would hear and run out to help her right away.

Not if they're sleeping too deeply, her mother's voice warned. No one heard Isla go missing in the night, and no one heard whoever had stolen their food, either.

She needed to stop thinking. She was freaking herself out.

A whimper and the sound of someone came from behind her, and her heart lurched. She twisted towards the tent. The front was open.

Ainslie.

Had someone got in there while Grace wasn't paying attention?

She jumped to her feet and rushed to the tent. "Ainslie?"

Panic and fear had heightened her voice, catching the attention of the others.

"Is everything all right?" Craig shouted after her.

She heard the movement of Fraser and Nicola climbing out of their tent and chasing after her, but she couldn't process what they were saying or reassure them right now. What if someone had got into the tent and had hurt Ainslie? She should have been sitting, facing the tent, not away from it. How stupid. She knew how quickly Scott had been killed.

She stuck her head through the open entrance, scanning the sleeping bags for their guide. The tent was empty.

Oh God.

The noise came again, and this time she realised it was from the opposite side of the tent. She rounded it to find Ainslie bent double. Grace sagged in relief from finding Ainslie there, unhurt, but then tensed again as Ainslie vomited a stream of hot water and stomach acid onto the ground.

"Are you all right?"

Ainslie gagged, a thin line of saliva hanging from her lower lip. She shook her head. "The water. I think the water must have been bad."

"It was boiled, though, wasn't it? And we've all drunk it. None of the rest of us are sick."

"I know." Her voice was croaky from vomiting. "The water in my bottle. I thought it tasted funny, but I thought it was just because it had been taken from the river."

Grace widened her eyes. "What are you saying? You think the water in your bottle was different to what we drank? You think someone switched it?"

"I don't know. I'm probably just being paranoid."

"You have every right to be, considering everything that has been going on."

She remembered seeing Nicola collecting water, how she seemed to have been walking fine, but then had started to limp the moment she'd spotted Grace. Surely Nicola wouldn't have switched the boiled water in Ainslie's bottle for some directly from the river? What possible reason would she have for doing that?

Something wasn't adding up.

"Is everything okay?" Fraser asked from behind them.

"Ainslie's sick," Grace told him.

Close behind Fraser was Nicola, and Craig was a little farther back, his nose wrinkled at the sight of Ainslie throwing up.

"Is she going to be okay?" Nicola asked, seeming genuinely worried.

"I'm sure she'll be fine," she replied, her tone curt. She found herself staring at Nicola, trying to spot any malice in the other woman's face. Why would she have done this? Maybe it had just been an accident, and someone had filled Ainslie's water bottle from the unsterile container?

Grace remained quiet for the moment, not wanting to accuse anyone for no reason. Maybe she was being paranoid, too, and the water Nicola had collected had nothing to do with Ainslie being sick now. She had no proof it was the water, or that Nicola had been the one to switch it. Ainslie could easily have eaten something that had upset her stomach, or maybe she'd even picked up a bug that had incubated for a while. There were numerous different possibilities. The last thing they needed was to start accusing each other. Craig had already been on the receiving end of how that had felt when they'd accused him of doing something to Isla, but then he'd been more than happy to shift the blame around to Malcolm.

Where was Malcolm now? If he was still alive, he'd have made it to the town and would hopefully have sent help.

She rubbed Ainslie's back while Ainslie dry heaved again. Grace tried not to wince. Poor Ainslie. That must be horrible for her. She hoped the rest of them weren't going to get sick as well.

She longed to hear the *whop-whop* of helicopter blades, the distant drone of an engine, that signalled a rescue team coming.

When Ainslie had finished throwing up, Grace helped her back to the tent.

"I'll get you my water bottle," she told Ainslie. "Drink from that if you think yours might be contaminated."

Ainslie curled back up on her sleeping mat, and Grace pulled the sleeping bag up to her chin. Her skin was ashy, and even though she felt cold to the touch, she was still sweating.

"Thanks for taking care of me, Grace."

"No problem. You need to stay hydrated, though, okay? Drink, even if you think you might throw it back up."

Ainslie nodded weakly. "I'll try."

Grace shot her a final concerned look and then climbed back out of the tent to join the others, who were all standing around the campfire, all with equally anxious expressions.

Fraser kept his voice low, so as not to disturb Ainslie. "How is she?"

Grace pressed her lips together and shook her head. "Not good. She thinks the water in her bottle might have come from the water that hadn't been boiled yet."

Fraser frowned. "How is that possible? We all shared out the water straight after it had cooled."

Grace flicked her gaze to Nicola, who seemed as worried as everyone else. Maybe Grace was overthinking this—it wasn't as though it would be the first time she'd jumped to conclusions and been wrong. "I have no idea. We're guessing, of course. It might be something else entirely."

Nicola lifted her face to the sky. "I hope a rescue team comes for us soon."

"Me, too. Tomorrow, Jack will be waiting for us with the minibus, and when we don't show up, he'll know something went wrong on the hike and send help right away. I'm sure they'll find us soon after that. We just have to get through the next twenty-four hours or so."

"I'm fucking starving," Craig complained.

"We all are, pal," Fraser said, apparently irritated by Craig's complaints. "There's nothing we can do about that. Be thankful you're not chucking your guts up like poor Ainslie."

Or missing, like your wife, or dead, like Scott, Grace wanted to add but didn't. Pointing out just what a hideous situation they were all in wasn't going to do anything to help.

Besides, she didn't think she could cope with another bout of Craig crying again.

Chapter Twenty

Grace was already exhausted by the time the sun began to set.

She knew some of that tiredness was from hunger, but there was nothing she could do about it. She could tell the others were feeling it, too. Everyone was snappish with each other. They might have survived the day, but none of them were in a good place, physically, emotionally, or mentally. Ainslie had only crawled out of the tent to throw up again, though there was nothing in her stomach except for the freshly boiled water Grace was making sure she drank.

The last of the light filtered from the sky.

"I'm going to bed," Nicola announced, getting to her feet. "Let's hope the rescue team are with us by morning."

"I hope so," Craig said. "I don't think I can handle another day."

Grace shot him a glare. "We might not have any choice."

"I don't much like the idea of having to sleep next to Ainslie, if she's going to be throwing up all night either," he continued to complain. "Couldn't she have gone back to her own tent?"

Grace balled her fists, pressing her blunt nails into her palms. It was taking all her strength not to lose her temper with him. "No, she couldn't. And you're not sleeping alone either. It's not safe."

He huffed out a breath of irritation. "Fine."

Grace needed to get away from him, if only for a minute.

With Fraser and Craig still sitting by the fire, she stretched out her stiff back and shoulders, and then made her way to the tent to check on Ainslie. The other woman was sleeping, but it didn't appear to be a restful sleep. Ainslie muttered and twisted her head back and forth, her eyelids fluttering. Grace placed her palm against her forehead. Her skin was feverish.

Grace's stomach knotted. Poor Ainslie. She remembered that she had some paracetamol in her bag. Bugger. She should have given some to Ainslie when she'd been awake. She didn't know how well Ainslie would have kept them down, but it might have helped a little.

Making sure she was prepared, should Ainslie wake, she flicked on her torch and delved into her bag. She located the small first-aid kit and opened it up. The packet of paracetamol—minus the two she'd taken herself and the couple she'd given to Nicola when she'd hurt her ankle—were still there, so she took them out. Something else caught her eye. She'd forgotten that she'd brought the penknife with her. She'd thought it might come in handy for practical things, like picking a stone out of the sole of her boot, or cutting a piece of string, but now she saw it as a weapon.

Taking both the painkillers and the knife out of the kit, she slipped both items under her sleeping mat for easy access. Hopefully, she wouldn't need to use either of them, but at least she knew they were there.

She suddenly realised Craig hadn't come into the tent. Was he still sitting by the fire with Fraser? She'd thought she'd heard Fraser join Nicola in their tent, and it wasn't safe for Craig to sit by himself. He was probably still sulking over having to sleep next to Ainslie. She remembered Ainslie suggesting that two of them stay up to watch over the others, but they'd forgotten all about it when she'd become ill. Maybe he'd decided to keep watch after all, but he shouldn't be sitting by himself.

It was dark enough for her to need her torch, so she picked it up and switched it on, making sure she didn't shine the beam directly at Ainslie. Letting out a long sigh, wishing she could just curl up in her sleeping bag and claim the oblivion of sleep for a few hours, she climbed back out of the tent and straightened. The embers of the fire were dying, but there was no sign of Craig tending to them.

A worm of worry coiled inside her.

"Fraser? Nicola?" she called, knowing they'd hear her through the tent. She didn't care if she might wake them. This was more important. "Have you seen Craig?"

Movement came from inside the tent, followed by the raspy whine of the zip being pulled down. Fraser's form appeared in the gap as he ducked his way out and then straightened. He held a torch as well, which he flicked on but kept pointed at the ground.

"Craig?" He frowned and then used his torch to illuminate the campsite in thick swathes of light, as though expecting to find Craig standing there. "I thought he was with you, lass?"

"No, I was checking on Ainslie. I thought he was with you."

"Ah, shite. I went to bed. I assumed he was turning in, too."

Nicola emerged, already bleary-eyed. "What's going on?"

"Craig's missing," Grace said.

Fraser gave Nicola a reassuring smile. "He's probably just gone to take a piss."

How long had she been in the tent before realising Craig wasn't coming in? Ten minutes? Less or more? It was hard to tell. She'd been preoccupied with taking care of Ainslie.

None of them could go to bed while Craig was missing.

Grace chewed at a dried piece of skin on her lower lip, picking at it with her teeth until she tasted blood. "We're going to have to look for him."

Nicola stared between Grace and Fraser, her eyes wide. "But...but what if there's a killer out there? He could be waiting for us, waiting until we separate and make ourselves vulnerable."

"We stick together," Grace said, "or at least within a few feet of each other. No one is going to try anything if they're outnumbered three to one."

Nicola shook her head. "I don't like this."

Fraser put his arm around her and gave her a squeeze. "I'm sorry, love, but Grace is right. We cannae no' look for him."

Grace offered her a tight smile. "And we can't leave you here by yourself. You're safe if you come with us."

Nicola made a strange noise, somewhere between a sob and a whine, and she pressed her hand to her mouth but then nodded in agreement. When she spoke, her voice was small. "I'll just get my torch."

They waited while she nipped inside her tent again and then re-emerged with the torch in hand.

"Ready?" Grace hoped Nicola was going to be okay getting around on her sore ankle. It wasn't ideal for her to be walking on it, but they really didn't have any choice.

Nicola nodded. "Ready?"

"Craig?" Grace called. "Craig, where are you? Answer if you can hear me. We're all worried."

She strained her ears as she listened for a reply that didn't come.

They moved forward, each taking a step away from the person next to them, so they covered more ground. They took turns calling Craig's name but got no response. A quick sweep of their torches showed that Craig wasn't down by the river, and, unless he'd successfully crossed it without any of them hearing, the only other option was that he'd gone into the trees. That he would have done so made sense to Grace. If he wanted to find some privacy to go to the toilet, then he might have figured it wouldn't hurt if he was quick.

Still, the thought of going back into the woods, even with Fraser and Nicola by her side, filled Grace with dread. Images flashed in her head—the shape of a person darting between the trees. Her hand covered in blood. A walking boot poking out from beneath a bush.

She pushed her fears down as far as they would go and kept walking, allowing herself to be swallowed by the surrounding trees. "Craig? Where are you?"

Fraser's and Nicola's voices sounded around her, calling his name as well. With every step, the distance between them seemed to grow.

Grace used her torch to light the way, sweeping the beam back and forth, simultaneously wanting to find Craig, so they could get back to the camp, while also not wanting to find him out of fear of what she would discover. Every one of her senses was on high alert, and she jumped at the slightest sound—the buzz of an insect too close to her ear, the snap of a twig under-foot, the distant hoot of an owl.

She swept the torch back across the ground and paused, her heart in her throat. Ahead of her, a dark mound rose out of the ground. Its identity was swallowed by moon-cast shadows, but instinctively she knew exactly what—or who—it was. Even in the edge of the torchlight, she could tell the pool of black slowly ebbing from the shape wasn't part of the ground.

The world swam away from her in a slow, dizzying circle, and she reached out a hand, perhaps hoping for support, and finding none.

"Craig?" She would have thought she'd have screamed, but instead her voice barely cracked from her throat in a harsh whisper.

Naturally, he could not reply.

Grace forced her shaking hand to point the torch in the direction of the body.

She let out a gasp and clamped her other hand to her mouth.

"Grace!" Fraser's shout was followed by heavy feet running towards her. "Grace? What's wrong? Did you find something?"

He came to a halt beside her, Nicola close behind. Their torches joined Grace's, giving them a better view of the body.

Craig lay sprawled on his back, his eyes wide and staring at the canopy above them. The way his head was tilted back exposed the pale skin of his throat and the huge gash across it that opened like a grin. The pool of black she'd seen around the body was clearly blood.

She recognised how he'd been killed from the description Malcolm had given of the body of the walker they'd found in the bushes. A single slash opening his throat—fast and silent. Enough to get the job done and let the body fall to the ground, and be able to walk away, knowing there would be no recovery, and the victim would never be able to tell the police anything about who had killed him.

Nicola let out a whimper and stumbled back again.

"Fucking hell," Fraser muttered.

Realisation hit Grace like a hammer.

"Oh God. Ainslie!"

They'd been so caught up in searching for Craig and finding the body that she hadn't given any thought to poor Ainslie lying defenceless back in the tent. What if the killer had done this deliberately? Luring them away from the camp so he could murder Ainslie?

She turned and ran, panic filling her and tears blurring her vision.

The front of the tent flapped open from where she'd left it that way when she'd gone to look for Craig.

What if the killer was in there right now?

What if I'm about to walk in on him? An unaccustomed rage rose inside her. *Then I'll fucking kill him myself.*

She leaned into the tent to find Ainslie right where she'd last seen her. There was no sign of whoever had killed Craig.

Grace collapsed to her knees, breathing hard. Beside her, Ainslie moaned and rolled slightly, but she didn't wake. The world shimmered around Grace as tears filled her eyes and dripped down her nose and onto the tent floor, creating a little damp patch.

They were losing control. There was only four of them left now, and one of them was so sick she could barely wake up.

Their only hope was that help would come for them before whoever the sick bastard out there was killed them all.

She'd never felt so alone.

At least Fraser and Nicola had each other, though she couldn't imagine how terrified they must be at the possibility of losing someone you loved in such a way. Grace had no one who would miss her, not really. Her dad was probably going to grieve her loss in principle, but when it came down to it, she was barely a shadow in his life.

She remembered the small penknife and reached under her sleeping mat to locate it. For one horrifying second, she thought the knife had gone and that the killer must have been in here after all and had taken it, but then her fingers closed around cool metal, and she pulled out the knife. She flicked it open and then clutched the handle tightly, keeping the blade pointed towards the opening of the tent.

She heard footsteps as Fraser and Nicola returned to camp.

"Grace?" Fraser called. "Is Ainslie all right?"

"Yes," she managed to reply, but her voice trembled. "She's safe. He's not here."

"We should leave," Nicola hissed to Fraser. "We should pick up our stuff and get the hell out of here."

They were trying not to be heard, she could tell.

Fraser had also lowered his voice. "We can't just leave. What about those two?"

"Fraser..." Nicola's tone was pleading.

"We'd be walking in the dark, Nic," he whispered back. "It's no safer than staying here. We just have to make it until morning."

The idea of hiking in the dark, with no supplies, and a killer stalking them must have been enough to convince Nicola to stay, as she didn't argue.

Shaking violently with terror, and not wanting to leave Ainslie's side, Grace huddled up next to her and wrapped her arms around her knees. What more could she do now except protect Ainslie and wait until morning?

Chapter Twenty-one

"Grace!"

An urgent, hissed whisper.

Grace jerked up, lifting her face from her knees. She tightened her fingers around the handle of the penknife, amazed she'd managed to keep hold of it. She swiped the side of her mouth against her shoulder, wiping away a dribble of saliva. Jesus, she'd fallen asleep. She couldn't believe she'd fallen asleep. The torchlight she'd been sitting by had faded. How much time had passed?

"Grace?"

That same hissed whisper. Who was that? Ainslie? No, Ainslie was wrapped up in her sleeping bag beside her.

Rustling came at the front of the tent, and Grace lurched backwards and jabbed the knife in the direction of the opening.

Nicola's pale face appeared in the gap.

Grace exhaled a shaky breath. "Jesus, Nicola. You just scared the life out of me."

Nicola glanced behind her. "Keep your voice down."

"What's going on? Is he here? Is the man who killed Craig out there?"

To her surprise, Nicola's eyes filled with tears. "Yes, he is."

"Did he hurt Fraser?"

"No, he *is* Fraser."

Grace blinked, certain she'd misheard. "What are you talking about?"

Nicola's eyes swam in tears, her already pale skin almost translucent in the torchlight. "It's my boyfriend. It's Fraser. He's the one who's been doing this."

Grace's jaw dropped. "Fraser? It can't be Fraser."

"Please, it is. I just saw the knife that killed Craig. It was hidden inside our tent. It had blood on it."

Her thoughts blurred. "No...I can't..."

"Think about it, Grace. Fraser and Craig were sitting together, and we both went to our tents. I'd thought Fraser had taken a little long coming to bed, and then he climbed in, and he was out of breath and a bit shaky. I saw him hide something, but he didn't think I'd noticed. When I checked, I found the knife."

"I can't believe..." But Nicola was right when she said Craig and Fraser had been sitting alone together after they'd gone to bed. Could Fraser really have killed Craig and then gone back to the tent as though nothing had happened?

"We have to go," Nicola urged. "He's going to come for us next. I know he is."

Grace's heart tripped a beat. She clambered to her feet but had to stay slightly ducked, so her head didn't press against the roof of the tent. This tent had been Craig and Isla's, and so offered more space than her single-person tent, but it was still cramped.

"Where... What...?" She was still struggling to put a cohesive thought together. This news had completely sideswiped her.

"He's dangerous," she insisted. "He's going to kill us. We have to get out of here!"

Grace glanced down to the sick, sleeping woman beside her.

"What about Ainslie?" she hissed. "We can't just leave her here. She's barely conscious. She'll die if we abandon her."

Nicola reached into the tent and grabbed Grace's arm. "He's going to wake up. We have to go."

Grace felt as though her feet were rooted to the ground, her legs had become solid marble. "I...I can't do that."

There was nothing on earth that would make her leave Ainslie, sick and defenceless, even if it meant having to face a killer.

"You have to! It's the only way we're going to live. The minute he wakes up, he's going to know that I know, then he's going to come for us."

"I'm sorry. I can't."

Nicola glanced over her shoulder and dropped her voice down another level. Panic lit her eyes. "Oh God. He's coming."

The rustle of a tent sounded, followed by heavy footfall.

Fraser? Could it really have been Fraser who'd done this? She'd hiked all the way back here with him and he hadn't laid a finger on her.

Nicola gave a whine of fear, shot Grace one final, desperate look, and then vanished from the front of the tent.

Feet thudded against the ground, fading as Nicola increased the distance between her and the camp.

"Where are you, ye fucking bitch." It was Fraser's voice, no mistaking it, and he sounded furious, like she'd never heard him before.

Grace sucked in a trembling breath and clamped her hand over her mouth to prevent herself from screaming. Tears prickled her eyes. What the fuck was happening here? How could Fraser possibly be the one who'd done this?

She thought back to when they'd been walking through the fog. It would have meant he'd been the one to kill Scott, so he must have passed her in the fog. She remembered not being sure where everyone was—dark shapes moving in the white. She'd been certain Malcolm had been ahead of her, but what about Fraser? Could she remember where he'd been? She'd been so disorientated, unable to pinpoint where sound was coming from, the fog doing something strange to the acoustics. Had she thought his voice had come from behind her at one point? Could he have been walking with Malcolm, and then just stopped and waited for her to walk past him, unseen in the white, to come up behind Scott and hit him with that rock? If so, then he'd hurt Isla, too, and he'd killed Craig and maybe even that man they'd found in the bushes.

A short distance from the tent came a roar of anger, and then a scream. He'd gone after Nicola.

Something—or someone—heavy crashed through the undergrowth, twigs and larger branches breaking. Grace pictured Nicola trying to escape into the woods, with Fraser chasing after her, the knife he'd used to kill Craig still bloodied and clutched in his hand.

Nicola wouldn't be able to outrun him, not with her bad ankle. She remembered her penknife. Maybe Nicola wouldn't be able to fight him off, but if it was two against one, and she was armed—if only with a little penknife—they would stand some chance. Otherwise, what would happen? He'd kill Nicola and then he'd come back for her.

Grace took a step towards the front of the tent, her legs shaking. The knife trembled in her grip, and she tightened her fingers around the handle. She had to be strong, and brave. It was the only way they were going to make it out of this alive. Tears of fear filled her eyes, and she blinked them away, needing to be able to see where she was going. Angry shouts ricocheted through the air, close enough for her to follow.

"I'll be back for you," she told Ainslie softly. "Okay. I'm really going to try. I'm so sorry."

She stopped talking, knowing it was going to only make her cry.

Grace grabbed her torch, her penknife still clutched in her other hand, and clambered out of the tent. She braced herself, half expecting Fraser to attack her the moment she stepped into the open, but nothing happened. No, the heavy movement of people was now some distance from the tent, heading towards the woods. It didn't sound as though he'd given up on finding Nicola. She didn't understand how he'd hidden who he really was so well. He'd even fooled Nicola.

Grace glanced at the sky. It was still dark, but the night wasn't as black as it had been, fading to a cobalt blue. Morning was on its way, though she didn't know if she'd be alive long enough to see it. But the burgeoning dawn meant she could just about see well enough to turn off the torch. She didn't have much choice. If she didn't, Fraser would pinpoint her location immediately.

Moving as quickly and quietly as she could, she took after the two people. Nicola had fallen silent, and Grace assumed she was hiding. With her bad ankle, she'd have known she'd be unable to run far and that sheltering somewhere would be her best option.

Fraser was less quiet. Heavy crashes signalled him barrelling through the bushes and undergrowth, and every now and then he shouted out "Nicola?" and "I'm coming for you," his Scottish accent thickening with his anger. Grace was happy for him to keep shouting. At least when he was making this much noise, she knew exactly where he was.

But where was his girlfriend?

"Nicola?" she dared to whisper as she stepped between the trees. "It's Grace. Where are you?"

"Grace?" A tentative voice came back to her. "I'm over here."

Grace turned towards the sound. She was still cautious about Fraser's location, though the thought of Fraser as some murderous psychopath still didn't sit right with her. But she couldn't deny what she'd heard. He'd definitely acted as though he'd happily kill his girlfriend.

She didn't know what she'd do when she found the other woman. There still wasn't anywhere they could go where they'd be safe, but at least they'd be together. Fraser wasn't a particularly big man, though he must be far stronger than he looked to have overpowered the others so quickly.

Surprise. He'd taken them by surprise. That was how they hadn't noticed any of the others being killed. They'd probably seen Fraser and just thought 'oh, it's only Fraser,' and before they'd had the chance to think anything else, he'd struck.

A hand suddenly shot out from behind a tree as she passed, fingers wrapping tight around Grace's biceps. A yelp of fear escaped Grace's lips, and then the hand was over her mouth, cold and clammy, clamped against her face.

"Shh." The hiss was right beside her ear. "He'll hear you."

She relaxed, but only by a fraction, and shook Nicola's hand from her face. Nicola let go of her upper arm as well and stepped away from the tree.

"What are you doing?" Grace asked, keeping her voice down. "We can't just stay hidden. It's going to be light soon."

"We don't have any choice. Either we hide or we run, and you said yourself that you won't leave Ainslie."

Grace listened hard, trying to get an idea of Fraser's position. Where had he gone? Had he heard them talking? She didn't hear anything other than the normal sounds of the woods at night and the distant burble of the river.

"There is another option," she whispered back. "We hurt him badly enough that he can't hurt us."

"We can't do that!"

Grace held up the penknife. "We can try."

Nicola's face was pale in the growing light, her freckles standing out in sharp contrast to her complexion. But she pressed her lips together and nodded. "I should do it." She put out her hand for the knife. "I was the one who encouraged him to come on this walk. I was the one who brought him into everyone's lives. I should be the one who stops him, too."

Grace hesitated, but the look of fierce determination in Nicola's eyes made up her mind. "Okay." She turned the knife around and placed the handle in the other woman's hand. "Let's make the son of a bitch regret ever meeting us."

Nicola nodded and lifted the blade to eye level, as though checking the sharpness.

Then she stepped forwards, and with her free arm, slammed her forearm into Grace's throat, forcing her back against the tree trunk she'd just been hiding behind.

The air burst from Grace's lungs as she hit the tree, Nicola's forearm wedged across her throat. The knife that had been in her hand only seconds earlier was now pointed in her face. Grace tried to jerk away, but the tip of the knife pushed against the skin right beside her eye. Nicola pressed too hard, and a prick of pain went through Grace, and a trickle of hot blood ran down the side of her face.

What the fuck is going on?

"I've got her!" Nicola called over her shoulder. "It was even easier than you said it would be."

The crunch of heavy footfall came towards them, and then Fraser appeared behind Nicola.

"Well done," he said to Nicola, a sly smile tweaking the corners of his mouth. "You're almost as good an actor as me."

Chapter Twenty-two

Grace's mind spun in a slow circle, threatening to pull in at the edges and plunge her into a deep, dark hole.

Fraser's thick Scottish burr had completely vanished from his voice. He was definitely English, though she couldn't quite place the accent—somewhere southern. Acting. He'd been acting this whole time, had moulded himself into a whole other person, and she'd fallen for it.

Who was he really?

He locked his gaze on her and smiled. He ducked his head in a nod, as though he was only just meeting her for the first time. "Hello, Grace."

Terror and confusion rooted her to the spot, though Nicola's arm still pinned to her throat and the knife pointed at her face also went some way to keeping her frozen.

"What the fuck is going on?" she managed to gasp.

Fraser—or whoever the hell he was—took another step closer, bringing him in line with his girlfriend.

"I can take it from here, Nicola."

Nicola didn't release her hold on Grace's throat, but the knife beside Grace's face wobbled. Nicola glanced over her shoulder to address Fraser.

"You promised me I could do this one," she said, a hint of a whine to her voice. "That was what we planned, remember?"

He seemed amused. "Do you really think I'm someone who can be trusted? You've seen what I've done already."

Her lower lip poked out, and the expression transformed her entire face. Grace had always thought of her as beautiful and mature and calm, but now she looked the opposite.

"That's not fair! You promised!" She shoved her arm harder against Grace's throat, as though taking out her frustrations on Grace.

Grace lifted her hands to try to tug Nicola's arm away, but Nicola was far stronger than she seemed. Besides, she still had the knife pointed at her face, and right now she was as terrified of losing an eye as she was her life. What an idiot she'd been. Fraser and Nicola were in on this together, and Grace had just handed her only weapon right over to them.

Fraser put his hand out to Nicola. "Come on, give me the knife."

Her face furrowed. "No."

A muscle beside Fraser's eye twitched. "Nicola...don't test me."

"You promised!"

He jerked his hand towards her. "Now."

Nicola whipped her head back around to face Grace, and for a second she was sure the other woman was going to stab her, but then Nicola exhaled a long, frustrated sigh, and her grip on Grace relaxed a fraction. Her lower lip pouted, but she handed the knife over to Fraser.

"Thank you," he replied and then flipped the knife over so the handle was in his grip.

He moved so fast, no one had the chance to react. One moment, the knife was in his hand, and the next it was swinging in an arc, directly towards Nicola's face, the silver blade sinking into her left eye.

The arm dropped away from Grace's throat, and she screamed and stumbled away. Her foot caught on an exposed root of the tree she'd been pinned to, and she fell hard, her teeth clacking together, every bone in her body jarring. But she hadn't been able to tear her gaze away from the sight of the woman with the penknife sticking out of her eye socket.

Nicola's screams echoed around the trees. Her hands fluttered over her face, not knowing what to do.

Fraser didn't leave her that way for long. He lunged for her again, taking hold of the knife and plunging it deeper.

The wet twist of the blade in the socket filled Grace's ears, and Nicola fell silent and dropped to the ground.

Grace didn't have any time to waste. It would be her turn next.

Chapter Twenty-three

I had enjoyed this one.

It almost seemed a shame it was coming to an end.

But all good things came to an end, didn't they? That was what people said. Grace reminded me of when I'd been younger, when I'd been able to take my time and savour them. It had meant a lot to me that she'd trusted me enough to open up to me, to tell me about her life. I'd been correct when I'd recognised the pain in her eyes. It hadn't quite been what I'd suspected—I'd figured a broken heart caused by a man—but I'd expected the man to be romantically involved with her.

Not to be her father.

In a way, it made this even sweeter.

I had fallen into a fatherly role around her, acting as though I'd cared. To have her trust me, only to betray her in the worst possible way, was like manna for the soul. If I even had such a thing.

I'd enjoyed having a partner this time, too. It had thrown a whole different angle on things. I'd always known it wouldn't last and her fate would belong to me by the end, but she hadn't needed to know that.

There were things I'd easily hidden behind during my youth. An easy smile and a handsome face went a long way to winning people's trust. But looks faded, and I'd always known there was no one people were less trusting of than an older man on his own. That was why I'd needed her.

We'd met at a book club.

An actual, 'read a book a month and talk about it' book club. Only this book club had a theme. Murder. It wasn't as good as the real thing, that was for certain, and I sometimes laughed at the ridiculous ways the authors described what it was like when someone died, but it was entertaining, a way to pass the time, and I was able to meet like-minded people. Well, maybe not completely like-minded, but I had been able to meet her. She was a little younger than me, but perhaps she'd recognised something in me, and I'd seen the same in her.

We'd gone for a drink after the book club one month. I'd jokingly asked her why she loved this genre of fiction so much, and she'd said 'research' without even cracking a smile. From there, the conversation had moved on to things like 'if you were going to kill someone, how would you do it?' Of course, I'd never told her the full truth about who I was and what I'd done, but I'd dropped enough hints to fascinate her.

I became her obsession, and with that obsession came loyalty.

I had no such loyalty.

She'd been here to serve a purpose, no more, no less. Like everyone else on this lonely planet, I only wanted her around for as long as she gave me pleasure.

She'd done well. But her time was over now.

All their time was over.

Chapter Twenty-four

Half blind with panic, Grace scrambled to her feet, kicking dirt up beneath her heels, and ran.

It was almost morning now, the sun about to bridge the horizon. She'd thought morning would bring safety, but instead it had only brought more horror.

She didn't even know which direction she was headed, only that she needed to put distance between herself and the man she'd known as Fraser Donnel. Air wheezed in and out of her lungs, an iron band constricting her chest. Her throat hurt from where Nicola had rammed her forearm against it, and blood from the cut beside her eye trickled down her cheek.

Fraser's shout chased after her. "It's just you and me now, Gracie. I'm coming for you."

There was laughter in his tone. He was enjoying this.

Grace ran.

Low-lying branches whipped her in the face and arms, drawing blood, but she barely felt it. Fallen leaves and twigs crunched underfoot, and more exposed roots, partially hidden in the detritus, threaten to trip her again. Her legs didn't feel as though they belonged to her. She hadn't eaten all day, and the lack of food, combined with the amount of adrenaline coursing through her system, left her weak and light-headed. She twisted her neck to look back over her shoulder, trying to see how close he was, but he wasn't there.

Even the birds seemed to have fallen quiet, the woods normally alive with birdsong at this time of day. Now everything was silent except for her heavy breathing and the pounding of her heart.

Where the fuck is he?

Had he taken a shortcut to get in front of her? She imagined him hiding behind a tree somewhere ahead, ready to spring out at her.

Where could she even run to? They were still a good day or two's hike from the nearest town. Even if she had a compass and a map, she didn't know how to navigate. She could easily end up completely lost out here, wandering around in circles, with no food or shelter. If Fraser didn't get her, then exposure and starvation surely would. What would be better? To allow Fraser to kill her, and for it to be fast, or to take days to die painfully?

What about Ainslie? Their guide was still lying in the tent, sick and defenceless. Had he given up on her and gone for easier prey instead?

She couldn't handle that.

Grace drew to a halt, her feet skidding in the mulch, and spun around in the direction she'd just come.

"Fraser!" she screamed. "Or whatever the fuck your name is! Where are you, you son of a bitch? I thought you were coming to get me. Well, here I am, you fucker!"

Maybe she'd finally lost her mind?

She wanted to draw him away from the camp. If she led him far enough away, perhaps Ainslie would be safe. Maybe Ainslie would survive long enough for help to arrive. Grace thought of Jack, how he and Ainslie had seemed the perfect couple, living and running their business together in such a remote part of Scotland, with, in the colder months of the year, only each other for company. This would destroy Jack. Not only would he have lost Ainslie, but he'd also lose his business. Why would anyone want to book a tour with a company whose entire group was murdered?

Ainslie had someone who would miss her. Grace had no one.

That was enough of a reason for her.

A crack of a branch to her right sent her running again. How far had she gone now? She had no idea. All her focus was on putting distance between Fraser and Ainslie. He was coming after her, though, she was sure of it. Even though it was hard to hear anything over the top of her own gasps for breath and the racket she was causing by her crazed race through the woods, she sensed his presence just as she had that first night, when he must have been standing over her tent, planning what he was going to do to her.

She burst out through the trees and stumbled down a muddy bank, her feet plunging into ice-cold water. She gasped at the shock of it but quickly recovered, managing to stay upright so she didn't get a full drenching.

Grace glanced over her shoulder.

No.

Oh no.

Her stomach sank, and tears of frustration and fear threatened. To her left were the tents.

She'd managed to run in a circle, and she'd brought Fraser right back to the campsite.

Grace hesitated for a moment. Should she go to Ainslie and make sure she was all right? Perhaps she would be awake now, and Grace could warn her about what was going on. Ainslie most likely had a knife of her own in her kit that Grace could use. It would be better if she had a weapon—at least then she stood some kind of chance.

But then crashing came through the trees. There wasn't time. Fraser would be here any second.

She set her sights on the opposite bank.

Not even bothering to use steppingstones, she waded through the river. Water poured into the inside of her boots and soaked her trouser legs. Each footstep grew heavier as she soaked up more water, until she felt like she was wading through mud. She used her arms like pistons, forcing herself forward. It was like being trapped in a nightmare, only this was very real.

She threw a backwards look to see Fraser burst out from the line of trees. He roared in triumph at the sight of her struggling through the river and jumped in after her.

Grace squealed in fear and renewed her efforts. She'd almost reached the opposite bank.

A sudden dip in the riverbed took her by surprise, plunging her almost waist deep. She cried out, feeling as though she'd left her stomach somewhere behind her, but she kept going. He was gaining on her now, his strength and longer legs making it easier for him to cross. The riverbed tilted up again, and the water grew shallower until it barely reached her shins. She was able to touch the other bank with her hands, and she grabbed clumps of grass and weeds and used her hold on them to drag herself to the other side. Then she scrambled up the bank and was onto the hill she'd hiked up when it had been the four of them going for help. When Scott had still been alive, and Malcolm had been with them, and she hadn't known Fraser was a murderous psychopath.

With a cry, she ran. But her boots were filled with water, her trousers soaked and slapping against her skin. As well as being exhausted and starving, she was also now freezing cold, and no matter how much she urged her body to move faster, it refused to comply.

Fraser had reached the other side of the river and was pulling himself up the bank. Grace forced herself to focus on where she was going, making her legs move. The top of the hill was impossibly far away, and even if she managed to reach it, what would she do then?

The solid weight of a full-grown man slammed into her from behind, sending her flying forwards. She landed heavily, her chin hitting the ground, her teeth snapping together. Pain exploded inside her mouth, and she tasted blood, and realised she'd chomped down on the side of her tongue. Not that it mattered. She wasn't going to be alive much longer to care.

Fraser climbed on top of her and flipped her over, so she was lying on her back, with him towering over her. He wrapped his fingers around her wrists, pinning her arms to the ground on either side of her head. His knees pressed onto her thighs, so he was holding her down with his full body weight.

"No, please!" Grace bucked and thrashed beneath him, but he didn't budge. "Leave me alone." She knew begging was pointless, but somehow, she seemed unable to help herself.

"Now, why would I do that, when I'm having such fun, Grace? Can't you see how I'm enjoying myself?"

Images of the deaths that had come prior to hers filled her mind. The knife sticking out of Nicola's eye socket. The back of Scott's head, the skull caved in by the force of the rock. The gaping gash in Craig's throat.

What was her wound going to be? How would she die?

"Please, just let me go. I won't tell anyone it was you who killed the others."

Shame poured over her at the way she was offering to let a man like him go unpunished, but they were just words. Empty words. They both knew how this was going to end, and it wasn't with them mutually agreeing to part ways.

His blue eyes seemed to turn a shade darker. "I think we both know that's not going to happen. I'm getting older, and I want to make sure my time here has really meant something."

"You've killed people!" she cried.

"And what greater power is there than that? To take someone's life. To extinguish a living being from the earth. Like putting out a candle with damp fingers. Pfft. Gone."

It was so surreal hearing this different accent coming from Fraser's mouth. Fraser—if that was even his name. She doubted it was. She felt as though she was meeting an entirely new person to the jovial, protective Scotsman she'd thought she'd got to know.

If it would do no good to beg for her own life, perhaps she could beg for someone else's.

"Kill me, then, but don't hurt Ainslie!"

He let out an exasperated sigh. "Oh, don't worry about her. She's going to die anyway. I'm not going to kill her. Killing someone who is barely alive isn't any fun. It would be over before I'd even get to see the fear in her eyes at the understanding of what was happening to her. No one is going to find her here. She'll most likely be dead by tomorrow."

Grace tried to yank her hands out of his grip once more, but it did no good. "No, don't say that."

"You don't need to worry, 'cause you'll be dead by then, too."

Struggling wasn't making any difference. Now she'd stopped moving, the cold leached any fight she had out of her.

"How could you have done this?" She thought to all the people he'd killed. "Isla, and Craig, Scott, even Nicola."

His upper lip curled in disdain. "Nicola was nothing."

"You planned this! You planned all of it."

"Of course," he told her. "Almost every step. I'd already mapped it all out. We'd intended for Nicola to hurt herself, knowing we'd need to take a shortcut. We both managed to steal the phones while everyone was sleeping, though I have to admit that it was risky. If we'd been caught then, the game would be up, though we'd have just looked like thieves rather than murderers. Getting you to discover the body I'd dumped a week ago was fun, too. I hadn't known if I was going to be able to manipulate you all enough to get you to go in that direction, and then you did. That fog coming in was a stroke of luck, too. I'd been thinking of killing one of the men overnight, and then convincing you to come back to the camp, but in the end, I hadn't even needed to be gone that long."

"Why one of the men? Why not me?"

She wasn't sure she wanted to hear the answer.

"You were special, Grace. Honestly, you reminded me of someone." He gave his head a slight shake. His eyes narrowed a fraction, and his gaze drifted away from her, as though he was remembering something in his past life. "No, not just someone. A couple of people. Women who were special in my life, at one time or another."

"Like Nicola, you mean?" she dared to say. She'd seen how that had turned out.

He barked a short laugh. "No, not her. She was merely a means to an end. People are suspicious of men on their own, especially older men. When I was younger, I could charm my way into a woman's life, but now I see the suspicion in their eyes. I knew it would be different if I was part of a couple, though. When women see a man with another woman, it makes them safe. With Nicola around, I was no longer a threat."

"So, you used Nicola just so you could get close to other women?"

"She knew what she was getting herself into. We arranged all of this together, or at least I did the organising, and she came along for the ride. She'd always been fascinated with death, you know, and then all these true crime shows they put on the television recently only made her more interested. It took some time, but eventually she admitted to me that she wanted to know how it felt to take another person's life, and so here we are."

"She didn't know you were going to kill her."

"True, but don't feel sorry for her. She wanted to kill you, remember? And she was more than happy to watch the others die."

"I don't want to die," she pleaded, suddenly finding the energy to renew her struggles. She meant it, too. She really didn't want to die. Perhaps she hadn't properly been living since her mother had passed away, but she would change all of that now.

If she was given a second chance, she'd make the most of it. She'd grip life in both hands and live it. She'd sell the house and go travelling, meet new people, and do all those exciting things she should have done when she was in her late teens and early twenties.

Grace was aware that she was praying, making a deal with some unseen force she wasn't even sure she believed in.

But if He did exist, He wasn't listening.

"Sorry, Grace. This is the end for you."

Fraser released her wrists, but the relief was short-lived. He moved his hands from her arms to her already bruised throat, both hands wrapping around her neck, fingers squeezing hard.

She tried to suck in a breath and couldn't, only a painful wheezing sound emitting from between her lips. She lifted her hands to batter at his shoulders, but she was aware of how weak her strikes were. She tried to go for his face, but he reared back, creating enough distance between them to prevent her trying to gouge his eyes out.

His fingers tightened around her throat, and she tried to breathe, but it was impossible. Her lungs burned painfully, her brain flashing on red alert—*oxygen, oxygen, oxygen!*

Fraser squeezed her airways down to nothing, and her eyes bulged. She flailed her hands against his shoulders, then tried to claw at the fingers around her throat, but it all felt hopeless.

"That's right, Grace," he said, his voice impossibly calm, almost soothing. "Just give in to it. It's easier this way. Peaceful. When I was a boy, my mother used to sing me to sleep. That was before I killed her."

His words registered in Grace's mind. He'd killed his own mother, and now he was killing her. She was dying.

"Do you want to hear what she used to sing to me?" Knowing she was unable to give him an answer, Fraser continued, "Now I lay me down to sleep, I pray the Lord my soul to keep. If I should die before I wake, I pray the Lord my soul to take. Do you know that one, Gracie? It's brought me a lot of comfort over the years. You're going to die now, you'll never wake up again, Grace. How does that make you feel?"

Everything was a blur. Buzzing filled her ears, the thump of her blood slowing in her veins. She wasn't sure she was even connected with this world anymore. But then she caught movement over his shoulder.

Was she hallucinating now? Was this how it felt to die?

Her vision tunnelled. Her mum's face filled her mind, smiling down at her, her eyes full of love, but also regret. It was going to be all right. At least she was going to be with her mum again. She was sad for everything she'd lost, the life she may have lived, but being back in her mother's arms would make everything okay again.

As so often happened during times when she'd needed help, she heard her mother's voice in her head.

Not yet, sweetheart. I love you, but it's not your time yet.

A scream of rage cut through her mother's gentle voice, but it wasn't a male scream. Was it her own? She didn't feel as though she was screaming. She wasn't even breathing. She didn't feel as though she was doing anything at all.

Floating. She was floating...

Grace had never expected death to be so peaceful.

A rush and blur of movement came from above her, and there was a hideous crack, and suddenly Fraser jerked to one side. Immediately, the hands around her throat loosened. He toppled off her, falling to the ground beside her.

Grace sucked in a painful gasp of air, her hands instinctively going to her neck.

Ainslie, her skin pale and sallow, stood over them, a large rock—much like the one Fraser had used to kill Scott—in her hands. Ainslie must have realised she was still holding the rock, and she released it, letting it drop to the ground.

Fraser groaned and rolled to one side. Ainslie must have hit him hard, but it hadn't been enough to kill him.

Ainslie fell to her knees, all her energy expended, but she managed to reach for Grace and help her up to sitting. Grace coughed and spluttered, still trying to fill her lungs with much-needed oxygen. Her head was clearing, though she felt dizzy and sick.

Grace could barely imagine how much strength Ainslie must have needed to summon to cross the river and save her. She must have heard Grace's cries and climbed from the tent, seen her and Fraser on the hillside, and realised what was happening.

Ainslie lifted her gaze to hold Grace's eye. "He won't stop."

Grace pressed her lips together and nodded. She understood exactly what Ainslie was telling her. Men like Fraser didn't just give up. He was injured, but they were still in the middle of nowhere, with no help at hand.

Fraser was crawling away, dragging himself through the dirt. He was weak, though, the blow to the head clearly disorientating him.

Grace's throat burned from where he'd strangled her, and it still hurt to breathe, but Ainslie was right. She couldn't let him escape.

She struggled to her feet. She was dizzy from the lack of oxygen, shaking with fear and adrenaline, but she set her sights on Fraser. He'd killed so many and would have killed her if Ainslie hadn't stopped him. He didn't deserve mercy.

He was crawling towards the river, back to the small bank they'd climbed up. She had no idea where he thought he was going.

Grace fought every instinct to run from the man who'd almost killed her. She didn't want to be anywhere near him again, but she had to do this. On trembling legs, she walked the short distance to where he'd managed to crawl. She stopped beside him. He barely seemed to register her presence, not even raising his head to look at her.

You fucking bastard.

Grace placed her foot against his rib cage and *pushed*. Still stunned from the blow to the head, he lost his balance instantly and tumbled down the bank. He landed half in and half out of the water, his arm and leg buffeted by the flow.

It wasn't enough.

Grace half climbed, half slid down after him.

A whine of fear crawled from her bruised throat, but beneath the fear was rage. He'd come here intending on killing them all, even Nicola—if that was her real name. Innocent people who'd only wanted to spend some time in the fresh air with other hillwalkers. How dare he! How fucking dare he!

She landed on him, her knee in his spine, and grabbed the back of his head. He was conscious enough to struggle against her. Blood and hair coated her palm, but she barely noticed. The river rushed and gurgled right beside them, her feet getting wet again, and she shoved his face under the water. It was no more than a few inches deep, but it was enough. Her arms shook as she held him down. His body went rigid beneath her, and he tried to push back up, but her utter fury had given her a strength she didn't know she had. She wouldn't let him go on to kill her, and then Ainslie. He'd done enough.

After this, there would be no more killing.

Seconds were like minutes, minutes stretching to hours. She thought he would never fall still, that they would be locked in this struggle for life for the rest of eternity, but then the power went out of his muscles. She suddenly found herself holding a lifeless body under the water, all resistance gone. But still she didn't release her hold. He'd tricked her so many times, how did she know this wasn't just him acting again. He might have relaxed on purpose, hoping she would let him go, so he could burst from the water and push her under instead.

She didn't trust anything. Didn't trust the passing of time or the floppiness of his body under hers. What was even real anymore?

But then she remembered Ainslie at the top of the bank and realised she must have been sitting here, holding Fraser's body under the water for ten minutes, or perhaps even longer. Her fingers had grown frozen and rigid against the back of his head, and she'd lost feeling in the foot that was submerged in the water.

Shock. She was in shock.

She snapped back to reality and yanked her hand off the back of Fraser's head. The flowing river had washed most of the blood from her skin, though she couldn't help thinking of Scott and how her hand had also been covered in his blood. Would she ever again be able to look at her own palm without thinking of death? She clambered off the body and out of the river. Fraser's position, with half his lower torso still on the riverbank, meant he stayed where he was, and wasn't carried off downstream. If there was a heavy rainfall, it probably wouldn't stay that way, but for the moment, at least she knew where he was.

He's dead, Grace. He can't hurt you or anyone else anymore.

Maybe that was true, but she'd seen enough horror movies to know sometimes they came back.

Forcing herself away from the body, Grace dragged herself up the bank to where Ainslie was lying on her back, her eyes closed.

"Ainslie?" Her voice was a mere croak. "Are you okay? He's dead. It's over."

Ainslie's eyelids fluttered, and Grace pulled Ainslie's head onto her lap, giving her a pillow of her thighs. The other woman was hot and clammy to the touch. She was still sick, but Grace had no idea how to help her.

Instead, she held Ainslie and let the tears of relief and shock and horror pour down her face.

Chapter Twenty-five

Thwack-thwack-thwack-thwack-thwack...

The noise was like a pulsing in the sky, distant at first, but growing closer and louder with every passing second.

Grace didn't know how long she'd been sitting in the same position, Ainslie's head cradled in her lap, her legs stiff beneath her. She'd completely lost track of time. But when she lifted her head towards the sound, she found herself squinting into a sun that was directly above them.

A rush of panic filled her, and she straightened to get a view of the riverbank.

She exhaled a breath of relief. Fraser's body was where she'd left it, his head and right side of his body still in the water, bobbing around with the flow of the river.

She felt numb, not just emotionally, but physically. All her reserves had been depleted. Her throat was incredibly painful, and, as she attempted to swallow and couldn't, she realised how dehydrated she was, too. She needed water, and if she needed water, then so did Ainslie.

"Ainslie?" A flush of cold fear washed over her. Was she dead? Had Ainslie died in her lap while she'd zoned out completely? What kind of person was she that she'd allowed Ainslie to save her life but hadn't even made the effort to get Ainslie water or back under any kind of shelter from the hot sun?

Grace suddenly remembered the noise she'd heard.

She kept forgetting her train of thought. Something was wrong with her brain. She didn't seem to be able to focus on anything, her mind flitting from one thing to another.

It was the shock, and exhaustion, and dehydration, and hunger. She'd nearly died.

The flutters of an old anxiety danced in her chest. What if Fraser strangling her had deprived her brain of oxygen? What if he'd done permanent damage? What if this was just what she was like now?

Her breathing came faster, panic threatening to take hold.

"Grace?" Ainslie's voice snapped her out of it, and she blinked down at her. "Grace? There's a helicopter. I can hear it. It's coming this way."

"What?"

Ainslie nodded weakly. "Yes, listen."

They fell silent for a moment, and the *thwack-thwack-thwack* she'd heard a moment earlier filled her ears. Ainslie was right. It sounded like a helicopter.

Ainslie managed to push herself to sitting, and she reached for Grace's hand and squeezed her fingers. "They could be looking for us," she croaked. "You have to make sure they see us."

Today was Saturday. They should have met up with Jack by now. Would he have sent a helicopter out to find them? Would it have located them this quickly?

It didn't matter, she decided. All that mattered was that they were saved.

Grace somehow managed to get to her feet. She craned her neck, peering into the sky.

"There!" Ainslie cried, pointing at the ridge of the hill.

Right above it, the body of the red-and-white helicopter came into view.

Grace didn't think she'd ever seen anything so beautiful.

"Here!" She waved her arms back and forth in the air. "We're over here!"

The helicopter was still at a high altitude, and it swept over the top of them. For a horrifying moment, she thought it hadn't seen them and would keep going, but then it banked back around and reduced its height.

"It's going to need to land on a flat part of the ground," Ainslie said.

She was right. Where they were was on a slope, but Grace didn't have the energy to walk any farther.

The pilot chose a spot near the campsite. As it landed, the wind caused by the rotor blades whipped against their tents, sending anything that hadn't been pinned down flying up into the air.

"Here!" Grace croaked, still waving. "We're over here."

The side of the helicopter opened, and the rescue team, in their red jackets and white helmets, climbed out. The team rushed over to help them, splashing through the river. One of them gave a shout and pointed towards Fraser's body and shook his head.

A man and a woman reached them, and silver blankets were wrapped around their shoulders.

"What are your names?" the female half of the team asked them, having to shout above the roar of the helicopter.

Unable to believe this was all over, and overwhelmed with emotion, Grace burst into tears. "I'm...I'm Grace," she managed to say, "and this is Ainslie."

"My name's Kate, and this is Russel," the woman introduced, gesturing to the male half of her team. "Is there anyone else here?"

"No one else alive," Grace sobbed. "It was Fraser Donnel. He killed them all. He tried to kill us, too."

The two members of Mountain Rescue exchanged a concerned glance with each other. Perhaps they thought she was delusional, but they'd find out soon enough that she was telling the truth.

The man, Russel, patted her shoulder. "It's okay, you're safe now. We've got you. Can you walk?"

Grace nodded. "I'm okay, but Ainslie is sick."

A stretcher was brought out for Ainslie, and the rescue team carried her onto it. Ainslie reached for Grace's hand, and she took it, walking alongside the stretcher, using it as support.

"What happened?" Grace asked. "How did you find us?

The woman, Kate, gave her a smile. "One of your team, Malcolm Currie, reported your group as being lost. He was able to give us a good idea of which area to search for you, which saved us a lot of time."

"Jack?" Ainslie asked weakly. "Does Jack know?"

"Her husband," Grace filled in.

"Yes, he knows. He reported your team missing as well, but since they were both in different locations, and giving us two different walking routes, it took us a little while to realise we were dealing with one missing group, rather than two. They're together now and waiting for you."

They crossed the river to the helicopter and were helped on board. Kate strapped Grace into one of the seats, and then the helicopter rotor blades began to spin again, and the chopper lifted off the ground.

The rescue team flew them back to safety, Grace never once letting go of Ainslie's hand.

Three Weeks Later

G race sat at a table in the window of the East London café, staring out at the street beyond. She fiddled with the silver bowl filled with sauce sachets, pulling them out and slotting them back in again.

She had no reason to be nervous, but still her stomach twisted into knots, and she had to consciously force herself to take deeper breaths.

What would these women be like?

A person connected them all—a person who was now dead. She hadn't fully understood when she'd received the email from one of the other women, asking for them all to meet. What did she hope to achieve from this? Why was she even here?

Maybe it was just so she could reassure herself that it hadn't been her. That he hadn't chosen her because she was weak or broken. She wanted to meet these other women and see that they were just normal people who'd caught the sights of a psychopath. She hoped they could show her there was a way to live without fear and paranoia clutching at her heart.

After she'd been rescued and taken to the Aberdeen Royal Infirmary, the police had needed to speak to her. She'd told them everything she knew, including her suspicions that Fraser Donnel hadn't been Fraser's real name and that he'd been pretending to be Scottish. Once they'd finished asking her questions, the police had gone away again but had come back some time later to fill her in on what they'd learned. As she'd suspected, Fraser Donnel wasn't his real name. He'd gone by a number of different aliases over the years and had been wanted as a person of interest for several murder cases, not including the three people he'd killed on the walk—Scott, Craig, and Nicola. Sadly, Isla's body hadn't been found, and they had no way of finding out exactly what had happened to her.

Maybe she had run away with a secret boyfriend after all.

Grace's father hadn't surprised her at all with his behaviour. Even knowing his daughter was in hospital, he hadn't been able to find the time to come and visit her in Scotland. He made promises to come to the house when she returned to London—which she agreed to, hoping he might have changed—but he'd cancelled, and she'd told him not to bother making another date. She wished it hadn't hurt as much as it had, but there was nothing she could do about that. It was just something she needed to learn to live with, like so many other things.

Despite all her promises to herself when she thought she'd been dying, Grace hadn't emerged from the experience into a brand-new person with a different attitude to life. She was back in the house where her mother had died, even more fearful than she'd been before. Going through what she had wasn't something she was just going to miraculously get over in a couple of days. Not only had she watched others die, she'd also killed a man. It had been self-defence, but that didn't make the acceptance of it any easier.

She *had* learned, however, that she needed to be kinder to herself. Maybe she wasn't going to get over this straight away, but that was all right, too. She was allowed to take the time to heal, even if it took weeks or months, or even years.

She was still in touch with Ainslie. It was the one good thing that had come out of all of this. She'd gone on the walk not expecting to make friends, not *real* ones, anyway, but she'd come out of it with a friend she could actually talk to. Ainslie was the one person who understood exactly what she'd gone through, and they talked on the telephone into the early hours—not only about what had happened, but also about meaningless stuff like television programmes and what they'd eaten for dinner.

It meant Grace no longer felt completely alone.

Ainslie and Jack hadn't yet decided what they were going to do with the business. Right now, the future of it looked uncertain. How many people would want to go on a walk where people had died? But then, the Scottish Highlands could be an unforgiving place, and while people didn't normally die by the hands of another walker, there were known to be casualties, and people still took on the challenge.

A waitress appeared beside her table, a notepad and pen in hand. "Are you ready to order?"

Grace threw her an anxious smile. "Oh, I'm just waiting for some...others to join me." She hadn't known how to refer to the two women. They were hardly friends, since they'd never met, and had only exchanged a handful of emails. But she didn't think she could have said 'fellow victims' or something similar instead.

The waitress, a young girl, barely out of school, dropped the notepad back into the wide pocket on the front of her apron. "Okay. Just give me a shout when you're ready."

Grace nodded and returned to fiddling with the ketchup packets.

The small bell above the door dinged, and Grace's heart lurched. She sucked in a breath and looked up.

Two women pushed their way into the café. They both cast their gazes across the array of customers, clearly searching for someone. One of the women was older—in her seventies, at least, with her silvery hair cut into a bob, and a slender figure—while the other appeared to be in her late forties and sported a mass of curls that had been partially clipped back from her face.

The younger woman, who Grace assumed to be Natalie Anders, spotted her right away, and gave her a small wave. Shakily, Grace pushed back her chair and got to her feet. She stepped out from behind the table to greet them.

When Natalie got a couple of feet from Grace's table, she threw open her arms. "Oh my God. Grace. Come here."

This woman, a stranger, but someone she was joined to through their experiences, pulled Grace into her arms. Grace found herself folded into the kind of embrace she remembered her mother giving to her when she came home as a teenager with her heart broken over something or another that had been so small and insignificant but had felt like the world had ended.

Natalie held Grace tightly, and tears of utter gratitude and relief welled up in Grace's eyes, and she pressed her face to the woman's shoulder and succumbed to silent tears.

The weight of a second hand touched her shoulder, and she lifted her head to see the older lady, Doctor Amy Penrose, smiling at her kindly, rubbing her back to offer the same kind of comfort.

Suddenly embarrassed, Grace untangled herself and swiped at her eyes with the ball of her hand. "I'm so sorry. I don't know what came over me."

Natalie guided her back to her seat and took the one beside her. "Don't be silly. We know exactly how you feel."

Tears threatened again, and she did her best to hold them back, her nostrils flaring as she stared down at her hands and nodded.

Natalie reached into her handbag and produced a packet of tissues. "Here. We thought you might need these."

Grace accepted them gratefully and took one out to wipe her eyes. "Thank you. I don't know what I was expecting when you said for us to meet, but I promise I wasn't expecting to react like that. I feel like I've done far too much crying recently."

Amy reached over the table and patted the back of Grace's hand. "It's good to cry. Holding in your emotions won't help you in the long run."

Grace had read both their stories in old newspaper clippings online, though the emails the two women had written her had contained brief outlines, as well. The man she'd known as Fraser had kept Amy Penrose locked in a cellar beneath his house, in the same space as he'd hidden the body of his own mother, and he'd made Natalie believe he was perfect boyfriend material before showing his true colours.

"You've both been able to live normal lives since..." Grace circled her hand in the air. "Well, you know, since *he* came into your lives?"

She didn't need to explain who 'he' was for them all to understand exactly who she meant.

Natalie smiled. "Yes, I'm married now, with two children. I'm not going to pretend it was easy. Kyle, as I knew him, definitely did a number on my ability to trust people, but I decided I wasn't going to let him control any more of my life."

"Thank you. The trust thing is going to be hard. I already struggled with trusting men after my dad walked out on me and my mum when she was sick."

Amy's voice was calm and soothing. "Grace, I've made my living writing about people like the man you knew as Fraser Donnel. He was Edward Swain to me, when I knew him as a boy. People like him don't come along often, thank God. Your chances of ever meeting someone else like him are extremely remote. I think you can go on and live your life without ever having to fear the same thing happening again."

Grace sniffed. "I hope you're right. I keep asking myself why I survived and so many of the others didn't."

"Survivor's guilt." She took Grace's hand. "It's perfectly normal."

"I went through it, too," Natalie said. "He killed my neighbours, and I beat myself up for a long time after, blaming myself for bringing him into their lives. But, after a while, I realised I couldn't be held responsible for something another person did. I couldn't control him. I hadn't known I'd ever needed to try."

"People like Edward—I mean Fraser—are masters of deception," Amy continued. "Their ability to make others like and trust them is what makes them so clever. No one ever suspects the happy, friendly person as the one capable of doing such horrible things. It's that which messes with your head so much as well—that if you can't trust the people who seem good in your life, who can you trust?"

Grace nodded and pressed her lips together. "And how do you get over that?"

"Time," Natalie said gently. "And finally realising there are good people around you who will support you." She exchanged a glance with Amy, who gave a brief nod. "I guess that's why we wanted to meet you, so that you know you're not alone."

"And there was something else, too," Amy said.

Grace looked between them. "There was?"

Natalie's expression grew even more serious. "We wanted to say thank you. You got rid of him, once and for all—"Her gaze dropped down, as though she was fighting tears of her own. "Neither of us need to be afraid anymore."

"We can't thank you enough for that," Amy said. "All we can do is be here for you, should you need us, Grace. Whatever it is, at any time of day, we'll be here for you, too."

Their kindness overwhelmed her. "I don't know what to say."

"You don't have to say anything at all, or you can pour out the contents of your heart, or you can meet us some way in between. We won't mind."

The young waitress reappeared beside their table, her notepad and pen back in her hand. "Are you ready to order?"

Amy smiled up at her. "Yes, I think we could all do with a nice stiff drink."

The waitress's face instantly fell. "Err...I'm afraid we don't sell alcohol. We're a café, and it's only nine-thirty in the morning."

Amy laughed. "Oh, shoot. In which case we'll have to settle for a nice cup of tea."

The waitress's shoulders dropped in relief. "Tea, I can do. Was that a pot for three?"

The doctor threw Grace a wink, and Grace found herself laughing. She couldn't remember the last time she'd laughed with another person.

She smiled up at the waitress. "Tea would be perfect."

About the Authors

MK Farrar is the pen name for a USA Today Bestselling author of more than thirty novels. 'Some They Lie' was her first psychological thriller, but wasn't her last. She's now the author of four thriller novels. When she's not writing, M K is rescuing animals from far off places, binge watching shows on Netflix, or reading. She lives in the English countryside with her husband, three daughters, and menagerie of pets.

To get a free copy of M K first physiological thriller, *Some They Lie*, you can sign up to MK's newsletter here, https://dl.bookfunnel.com/6gbuu2gdl6 or check out her face-book page, https://www.facebook.com/MKFarrar.

She can also be emailed at mkfarrar@hotmail.com. She loves to hear from readers!

M A COMLEY IS A NEW York Times and USA Today best-selling author of crime fiction. To date (Dec 2019) she has over 100 titles published.

Her books have reached the top of the charts on all plat-forms in ebook format, Top 20 on Amazon, Top 5 on iTunes, number 2 on Barnes and Noble and Top 5 on KOBO. She has sold over two and a half million copies worldwide.

In her spare time, she doesn't tend to have much, she enjoys spending time walking her dog in rural Herefordshire, UK.

Her love of reading, and specifically the devious minds of killers, is what led her to pen her first book in the thriller genre she adores.

She has also started writing in the cozy mystery genre.

Facebook.com/Mel-Comley-264745836884860

Twitter.com/Melcom1

Bookbub.com/authors/m-a-comley

https://melcomley.blogspot.com

Printed in Great Britain
by Amazon